"I don't understand," Lacey complained

Damon leaned forward. "By tomorrow morning, Lacey, your parents will be thrilled to death that you are going to be sleeping with me."

His words had the harsh ring of truth and terrified her, even though she didn't understand what he meant. It hadn't exactly sounded like a threat, and yet—

"Do you mean you'd actually tell them you'll only buy Dad's hotel if I—" Her voice gave out.

"Oh, no. I'm not an idiot, Lacey. I do respect your father and I don't think he'd agree to the trade. But surely you remember there's a minor legal maneuver that will satisfy all their questions?"

He picked up his cup and saucer, looking at her over the rim, and said deliberately, "It's called marriage."

Leigh Michaels cannot remember a time when she was not writing—before she was old enough to print, she was dictating to her older sister. She graduated from Drake University at the top of her class and worked as a newspaper reporter, radio news director, public relations director and research librarian, all of which have provided her with valuable background for her romance novels. She has also taught creative writing at a junior college and has published a textbook on the subject. Her magazine articles have been published in *The Writer*, *Writer's Digest* and other publications. She is married, with two children who have left the nest, leaving her with her photographer husband, a lovable Siamese cat and her faithful mutt Charley. She currently lives in Ottumwa, Iowa, Radar O'Reilly's hometown and enjoys traveling to research her novels.

Books by Leigh Michaels

HARLEQUIN PRESENTS
1028—BRITTANY'S CASTLE
1049—CARLISLE PRIDE
1068—REBEL WITH A CAUSE
1107—CLOSE COLLABORATION
1147—A NEW DESIRE
1162—EXCLUSIVELY YOURS
1245—ONCE AND FOR ALWAYS

HARLEQUIN ROMANCE
2951—STRICTLY BUSINESS
2987—JUST A NORMAL MARRIAGE
2997—SHADES OF YESTERDAY
3010—NO PLACE LIKE HOME
3023—LET ME COUNT THE WAYS

LEIGH MICHAELS

with no reservations

Harlequin Books

TORONTO • NEW YORK • LONDON
AMSTERDAM • PARIS • SYDNEY • HAMBURG
STOCKHOLM • ATHENS • TOKYO • MILAN

Harlequin Presents first edition May 1990
ISBN 0-373-11266-1

CHAPTER ONE

EVEN though Lacey had been home for more than two weeks, it was still a bit of a shock each morning when she woke up in the bedroom of her childhood. The room had grown with her, of course; it was no longer pink and ruffled, as it had been in her babyhood. Still, Lacey thought as she luxuriously stretched and sat up, pushing the brightly striped sheet aside, it represented the teenager she used to be, not the grown-up, professional woman she was now. Something a little more sophisticated was called for. She yawned. Peach and moss green, perhaps— she'd mention it to her mother, and see what Ginny thought about redecorating. If she was going to live here, after all...

Then she remembered how much business she had left unfinished on her desk the night before, and she scrambled out of bed with a groan. That's not a good sign, Lacey Clinton, she scolded herself as she stood under needles of hot water in the shower. You've only been on the job two weeks, and you're already starting to feel as if the honeymoon is over!

But it wasn't really that, she tried to convince herself as she dug into her wardrobe for an oyster-white business-suit. She was enjoying her new job; public relations was what she was trained to do, and she had always wanted to be a part of the hotel. She was only feeling dis-couraged because it was such a lot of work just now. The hotel had never had an official public relations de-partment, so she was creating her own job from scratch,

7

in a sense. Once everything was set up, she told herself, she would love it.

At least, I'd better, she warned sternly. Because if I don't, I've got no idea how I'm going to break the news to my parents.

She brushed her long red-gold hair into a flaming stream over her shoulders, and tied the silky bow at the neckline of her salmon-coloured blouse. There would be plenty of time to worry about breaking the news to Bill and Ginny Clinton, she told herself, if and when she decided not to stay. And that probably wouldn't happen. After all, she loved being back in Kansas City—after two years in the mad race that was Manhattan, coming back to her home town was heaven. She had missed the easy pace, the almost small-town friendliness of the people here. She certainly would never catch herself saying that she missed the pace of New York! And, of course, there was the hotel.

The Clinton Hotel was in her blood, just as it was her father's pride and joy. Some day she would take his place as general manager and owner, as he had planned from the time she was a child.

And there is no sense in feeling queasy about it, she told herself firmly. Of course it looks like a bigger job now than it did when you were ten years old. But by the time Dad's ready to retire, you'll be eager to take over.

After all, she reminded herself, that had been the dream of years, her plan as well as her father's, until one man and her own naïve heart had blasted her life into shreds two years ago, and sent her running to Manhattan instead——

Well, she told herself sternly, none of that mattered any more. Even though she had believed at the time that her heart was forever broken, it had been foolish to allow herself to get sidetracked from the paramount goal—the hotel. Giving up everything that really mattered to her because of a man—it had been a childish thing to do. But now she had come to her senses, and Lacey Clinton was home to stay.

She squared her shoulders at the thought of the paperwork that was waiting on her office desk, and went down the broad stairs of the rambling frame house in Hyde Park.

Her mother was humming an old love song as she cleared the evidence of Bill Clinton's breakfast from the table. 'Good morning, darling,' she said cheerfully. 'What would you like for breakfast?'

'Just toast and juice, please.' Lacey kissed her mother's cheek and reached for the coffee-pot. 'And I can get it myself, remember? You're not supposed to be waiting on me.'

'But you can't possibly work all day on only a slice of dry bread. I'd much rather you would——' Ginny stopped in midsentence and smiled ruefully. 'When you agreed to move back in with us, I promised not to act like the mother of a teenager, didn't I?'

'You did,' Lacey agreed, with a smile.

'And here I am nagging you about what you eat——'

'I'll forgive you this once.'

'I hope you don't run out of forgiveness soon,' Ginny Clinton admitted, 'because I've a feeling I'm going to need it. Oh, Lacey, it's just so good to have you home! I'm black and blue all over, I've pinched myself so much—I can scarcely believe you're real.'

Lacey spread apricot jam on her toast and said, 'That's flattering. But has anyone ever told you that you might be prejudiced about your only child, Ginny Clinton?' She settled herself at the breakfast-table and spread a linen napkin carefully across her pale skirt. 'Has Dad already gone to work?'

Ginny nodded. 'Half an hour ago. But he said to tell you not to be concerned about when you got there.'

'That's a switch from my last boss.' It was only a murmur. In a way, Lacey thought, I wish he'd be tougher on me. Treat me like any other employee——

'He's so glad to have you home,' Ginny said softly. 'It's going to be such a help to him to have you here. You know, Lacey, he hasn't been feeling as energetic these last few months.'

Lacey set her cup down and stared at her mother in shock. 'He hasn't breathed a word about not being well.'

'He wouldn't. And he actually hasn't been ill—he just gets tired out sometimes. Having you in the office will take a great deal of pressure off him.'

It almost sounded like a warning, Lacey thought. But that, surely, was only because of her own uncertainties about the job she was tackling.

'You're not going to work so late tonight, are you, Lacey?' her mother asked diffidently. 'Don't forget that I asked George and Elinor to come for dinner. They haven't had a chance to see you since you got home; you've been working such long hours——'

Lacey propped her elbows on the table and smiled across at her mother.

Ginny sighed. 'I'm doing it again, aren't I?'

'Well, yes. I think we might as well give it up, Mother—you're not going to be much of a success as a mere landlady, taking no personal interest in the tenant. If I happened to stay out all night——'

'I'd be pacing the front hall with a candle,' Ginny agreed. 'Just as I did when you were sixteen.'

'I was seventeen. And I'll never forget the tongue-lashing I got. Not that I'm planning on staying out all night again, but——'

'Well, I should hope not! What on earth could a young woman be doing but getting into trouble, running around at all hours of the night——?'

'Precisely. You told me that a long time ago.' Lacey pushed her coffee-cup aside and said lightly, 'I'm going to go and be a help to my father.'

Ginny looked abstracted. There were two fine lines in the middle of her forehead, Lacey noticed. They looked like worry lines. Funny that she hadn't seen them before. Was it Bill Clinton, or Lacey herself, or something else, that was worrying Ginny?

Well, there wasn't much she could do about the other things, but she could at least reassure Ginny about her own state of mind. 'Mother?' She bent over Ginny and gave her a hug. 'Don't take me seriously. I'm not going to throw a tantrum because you want to know where I am, you know—I'm not fourteen any more, and I know that adults can ask about each other without being nosy.'

Ginny smiled. 'Of course, dear,' she said gently. As Lacey left the room, she was already clearing the table.

But that look on her mother's face stayed in Lacey's thoughts all the way from the house in Hyde Park to the big hotel downtown. It had been almost an absent expression, as if there was something else nagging at Ginny's mind.

She was probably just wondering what to serve for dinner tonight to keep up with Elinor's gourmet cooking, Lacey told herself crossly as she reached her office. And, even if that wasn't it, if you go prying into her thoughts, you're the one who's being nosy. Honestly, Lacey, you're starting to see trouble lurking in every corner!

Her desk was still piled high. What did you expect? she asked herself as she took her jacket off. That little elves would have taken care of it all overnight?

The public relations office of a big hotel covered an enormous amount of territory—especially, Lacey told herself, when the general manager considered it as a training ground for his successor. For instance, the supply of promotional brochures was exhausted, but before the printers could do another batch the whole thing would have to be reorganised. The room service menus needed to be overhauled by yesterday, and there was a stack of mail and messages on her desk six inches thick. Had no one been doing any of this stuff? she asked herself helplessly three hours later, realising that she had made only a small dent in the pile.

Just then her father popped his head in the door. 'Lacey, my girl, let's go and have lunch.'

She shook her head, eyes still on the letter that she had just opened. 'I really can't, Dad——'

'It's the monthly tourist board meeting,' Bill Clinton said gently.

Lacey sighed. There were several groups in the metropolitan area that promoted and co-ordinated tourism. Attending their meetings was certainly part of her job. But why did it have to be today? she wondered irritably. She put the letter down and looked up at her father.

Was his health a matter of concern? He didn't look ill, Lacey thought. Bill Clinton was greying now, but he was still trim and fit and bronzed, nearly as handsome as the photographs of three decades ago, when he'd been a very eligible bachelor as well as the general manager of the grandest of Kansas City's old hotels. That, of course, was before the day a young woman guest had stormed into his office wearing a terry-cloth bathrobe to complain about a lack of hot water in her room, and Bill Clinton had lost his heart to Ginny...

Lacey had heard the details a thousand times; it had been one of her favourite bedtime tales as a child. Hotels, she thought. This one brought my parents together, and I'll spend my life in it, one way or another.

A trickle of sadness oozed through her at the memory of the way the hotel had shaped her parents' lives. Once she had thought that she, too, had found her love here inside the hotel. But that was not to be.

What's the matter with me? she asked herself. Why am I even wasting time thinking about Damon? I got over him long ago, or I would never have come back here. At the time I thought I would die because he didn't love me, but I survived. And he's got no place in my life now, that's for certain—not even the space of a thought.

'Well?' Bill Clinton asked.

It took her a minute to remember the luncheon. 'All right. Give me a minute to comb my hair.'

He grinned. 'Combed or not, Lacey, you'll be the hit of the party. You're certainly the prettiest thing that's turned up at the tourist board meetings in a year.'

'That wouldn't be hard,' she retorted.

She raised an eyebrow when they reached the hushed elegance of the Clinton's green and gold lobby and he turned towards the street entrance of the car park. 'The board meeting is at the Kendrick this month. We sort of take turns among the hotels.'

Lacey didn't say anything. The late summer heat caught at her breath as she stepped on to the pavement, and the lunchtime crowds made a good excuse not to talk.

She looked up at the massive stone tower of the Kendrick Kansas City, across the street and down half a block from the Clinton. Like the Clinton, it, too, was an old building, but careful cleaning had restored an almost-new gleam to the carved and sculptured façade. She hadn't been inside it in two years...

You'll have to do it some time, she told herself. It might as well be now.

The heat radiating from the pavement made it hard to get her breath. I'm just not used to it yet, Lacey thought. It gets hot in New York sometimes, but not like this...

'It was closed for nearly a year, you know,' Bill Clinton said. 'Damon poured a ton of money into it. I think he replaced everything from basement to penthouse, just for the sake of changing it.' He gave a push to a gleaming brass revolving door and ushered Lacey through.

Not everything, surely? Lacey thought. I remember this door. I nearly walked into the edge of it that night, when I couldn't see for the tears...

'He wanted me to do the same thing, you know. Together we could anchor the whole convention centre business, he said.'

'I didn't know that,' she said.

'Not my kind of risk,' her father went on. 'It's all right for him—he's got forty other hotels keeping the cash-flow going and helping to support a job like that. Even if he decided to do it all over again next year, it would scarcely make a ripple in the bottom line of his balance sheet.'

Change for the sake of change—— Yes, Lacey thought, I can see Damon doing that. Damon never liked to settle for one thing when he could have a choice. But he would also never forget about the profit margin, for the chain of hotels his company owned, or for himself...

'Still,' Bill Clinton said, almost as if he was talking to himself, 'sometimes I wonder if I should have done it.'

'The Clinton's doing just fine as it is.'

Her father looked down at her with a fond smile.

'We're a little hotel with a loyal clientele,' she said stoutly. 'What's the point of changing it?'

She braced herself for a shock as she walked across the outer foyer and stepped into the high-ceilinged grand lobby of the Kendrick Kansas City. It had never had the sheer splendour of the Clinton's lobby, but still she would hate to see it destroyed. What would he have done to it? she wondered. Installed a fast-food restaurant? Knocked a hole in the wall so guests could drive in to register?

Her first impression was of the things that had vanished. Gone were the heavy red velvet draperies that had closed off each archway into the lower halls and hushed the sound of travellers' footsteps. Gone were the mirrored doors that had shut off the upper balconies. In their place was open air and cool blue and grey furnishings—and people. What had been a cold and formal and quiet—always quiet—room was now filled with soft music from a grand piano in the centre of the lobby, and with a comfortable buzz of conversation as groups gathered here and there, waiting for tables in the nearby restaurant. That was new, Lacey thought. Or had it always been there, so well-hidden behind those red velvet draperies that only an intrepid explorer could find it?

She looked thoughtfully out over the room as the escalator carried them up to the mezzanine, to the meeting-room where the buffet luncheon for the tourist board had been set out. The remodelling of the Kendrick Kansas City had been change for the sake of change, her father had implied. But if that crowd down in the lobby was a sample of what Damon had done to the rest of the hotel——

I'd like to ask him about it, Lacey thought. I'd like to know by what percentage it increased the occupancy rate, and what return he figures he's getting on the investment.——

Purely business questions, she realised with a tinge of relief. Questions asked of a business colleague. Good, that meant that she'd been simply shying at shadows on the way over here. Damon Kendrick had flicked her pride two years ago, but he hadn't really wounded her heart, after all. And so she could face him again, at the tourist board meeting or anywhere else, without fear.

He wasn't at the luncheon. That was not surprising, Lacey told herself; the Kendrick Kansas City was the flagship and headquarters of the chain, but Damon himself might be in Seattle or Boston or Nassau, or any of the other thirty cities in which Hoteliers, Inc. owned or managed hotels.

She assembled a sandwich from the lavish spread on the buffet table, filled a bowl with a hearty-looking vegetable soup, and joined her father at the big square table. A couple of minutes later a young woman came over to join them, juggling a soup bowl and a portfolio. 'So the adventurer finally came home,' she murmured as she pulled out a chair.

Lacey jumped up. 'Julia!'

Julia Patterson fended off a hug with a grin. 'Watch out for the soup!'

'What are you doing here?' Lacey asked, a little guiltily. Surely she should know; she and Julia had been best friends in college. But in the last two years she'd lost track of most of her old friends.

'Don't remind me,' Julia murmured. 'I'm the executive secretary of this organisation now.'

'In other words, the boss.'

'Well, that's what they told me when I took the job, but I think it really means that I take orders from everyone. Are you truly home to stay this time? I heard you've already settled in at the Clinton, and a new public relations office must mean that the hotel is finally going to take a more active part in the tourism promotions we're planning——'

A more active part? Finally? Lacey wanted to ask what Julia meant, but, before she could swallow her bite of ham-on-rye and phrase the question, the president of the organisation had called the meeting to order.

It was more than an hour later, as the meeting broke up, that she got a chance to ask, and the answer left her chewing her bottom lip.

'The Clinton doesn't seem to be getting the sort of response from clients that we would all like to see,' Julia said flatly. 'I think if you'll look over the balance sheet you'll see what I mean.'

That left Lacey confused. Just how would Julia know what the Clinton's balance sheet looked like? But, before she could ask, Julia looked around and said, 'I suppose your father has introduced you to all the new people——'

'Haven't had the chance,' Bill Clinton said as he pushed his chair back. 'You know them all better than I do, anyway, Julia.' He smiled. 'I need to run downstairs to talk to the head of catering for a minute. I'll wait for you in the lobby, Lacey.'

'See?' Julia said without rancour. 'I take orders from everyone. Have you met Grant Collins? He's the general manager of the Kendrick Kansas City now.'

Lacey shook her head. 'I'm shocked by how much turnover there has been in the industry since I left.'

'There's been a string of general managers here in the last few years, that's certain. Grant's survived longer than most.'

'It would be a challenge to work for Damon, I'm sure.' It was absent-minded; Lacey was watching the man Julia had pointed out across the room, and she didn't see the quick look the young woman gave her.

'It's especially tough here, with Damon's office right up on the sixteenth floor. Some of them seemed to forget that the general manager of a hotel is the boss, and they kept running to Damon with every minor problem. They didn't last long.'

Lacey finished her inspection of Grant Collins—a tall, nice-looking, athletic type who looked confident of himself, she thought—and turned back to Julia. 'And others just quietly got ulcers because they thought the chairman of the board was watching their every move,' she said drily. 'Which, of course, he was.'

'Something like that. Have you seen him since you came back?'

'Damon? Why would I? It's long over with, Julia.'

Julia didn't answer. 'Come on and I'll introduce you to Grant. You two really should know each other.'

Yes, we should, Lacey thought idly. It would be interesting to compare notes on how we've both managed to survive a few months of close contact with Damon Kendrick . . .

Close up, Grant was even better-looking, and his blue eyes were frankly interested at his first sight of Lacey. His handshake was firm and warm, his light brown hair was pleasantly curly and his smile was engagingly crooked.

That's part of his success, Lacey thought. I'll bet he can charm the dowagers right out of their bad moods. But he can't be as innocent as he looks, or Damon would have chewed him up by now.

'Thanks, Julia,' he said, still holding Lacey's hand after the introductions were over. 'You've just made the hotel business in this city a hundred per cent more interesting.'

Lacey laughed at him and retrieved her hand. 'Perhaps we should have coffee some time and discuss occupancy rates.'

'How about making it champagne, and we can talk about the colour of your eyes?' he countered smoothly.

I was right, Lacey thought. He's definitely not innocent. But it was flattering, nevertheless, and she felt a little stir of interest. She might be living with her parents, but that didn't mean she wanted to be a hermit, and it was always pleasant to be told that she was attractive. 'Coffee,' she repeated gently. 'You know where to find me.'

Grant laughed. 'You win,' he said. 'We'll start with coffee.'

Julia gave Lacey a long, appraising look as they crossed the half-acre of pale blue and grey carpet on the mezzanine to the lobby escalator. 'Lacey, I've never seen men act that way, except when they're around you.' Her tone was good-natured, but there was a note of seriousness underneath. 'I always have thought you were some sort of witch when it came to men. It's enough to make even your best friend jealous.'

'Sorry.'

'No, you're not. There's your father. Shall we go down?'

Bill Clinton was leaning against a marble pillar at one side of the big room, his arms folded, watching the parade of people. What was he thinking? Lacey wondered, and let her eyes sweep over the lobby. The view from the mezzanine was a wonderful vista, she thought. Taking those doors out had been a brilliant idea. And as for the long, open lobby escalator—what a glorious way to make an entrance, and grab the attention of a crowd——

Out of the corner of her eye, she saw a tall, dark-haired man come into the lobby from the direction of the street. There was no reason she should have spotted him, one man in the middle of a stream of humanity. But she did. He was wearing a pale grey suit, and under his arm was a slim leather portfolio. He seemed to be alone, and as she watched he stopped in the doorway, his head up as if he was testing the scent of the room, his eyes roving. It looked like a habitual gesture.

I wonder if he does that every time he walks into one of his hotels, Lacey thought. As if he's sniffing for trouble.

His gaze came to rest on the escalator just as Lacey's foot settled firmly on to the top step, and then it was too late to turn back. Her heart started to thud violently, and her fingers clutched the railing. For a long moment, he stood at the end of the lobby and watched while the escalator carried Lacey inexorably downwards towards him.

It's all right, she told herself. You have to meet him some time. Just take a firm hold on yourself, and be charming and polite, as if you've forgotten everything that happened two years ago.

'All over, hmm?' Julia said drily. 'Damon is standing there staring at you as if he's about to start drooling.'

Lacey exerted every ounce of strength she possessed and turned to look at Julia with a light laugh. 'Damon has far better manners than that—he would never drool in public.'

Damon Kendrick looked up for one endlessly long moment, in which Lacey felt as if the escalator had travelled miles instead of mere feet, and then he strode across the lobby and vanished in the direction of the reception desk.

Lacey wasn't quite sure whether she felt relieved or disappointed that the inevitable meeting had been avoided for the moment. After all, she would have to face him some time.

'Witch,' Julia said succinctly, just as the escalator reached the bottom, and Lacey laughed.

'A very successful witch, wouldn't you say?' she murmured. 'I certainly made him vanish in a hurry.'

'I may just turn a few of these things over to you,' Bill Clinton confided as they returned to the hotel. 'The boards and committees and such. You seemed to enjoy it. I'm getting a little too old to be patient with the process.'

'You, old? Never, Dad.' But it was true, she thought. He was almost sixty. And by the time he retires, I'll be more than ready to step into his shoes, she told herself. I have to be.

The Clinton's doorman, in his bottle-green livery with the gold braid on the sleeves, touched two fingers to his hat as they approached. He was new, too, Lacey realised; at least, she hadn't seen him on duty before. It was startling how many of the people she remembered at the hotel had retired or moved on in the last two years. But apparently the Kendrick had similiar problems—at least when it came to general managers.

That should be no surprise, she told herself. Damon must be dreadfully hard to work for, with that arrogant certainty of his—the conviction that he was always right. She had to admit, though, that when it came to the remodelling of the Kendrick Kansas City he'd been absolutely correct. What had been a mildly profitable mid-sized hotel now appeared to be a stunning success.

That sparkling blue and grey lobby had looked like a small jewel of a watercolour sketch, she thought. And in comparison the Clinton's green and gold now looked to Lacey like a sombre old oil painting, dark with age and a bit tattered at the corners, in a dusty, tarnished frame.

It's your imagination, she told herself, and went back to her office to check on the balance sheet, as Julia had suggested she do.

She had thrown down her pencil and was staring out of the window at six o'clock when her father knocked on her door. 'Lacey, your mother's expecting us,' he reminded gently.

Reluctantly she turned her swivel chair around, and obediently started to clear her desk.

'May I hitch a ride with you?' he asked. 'I let one of the boys take my car this afternoon.'

'Sure.' She locked the papers she'd been working on in the drawer of her desk and got her handbag.

'You're awfully quiet,' he said.

'I'm thinking. It's been a long afternoon, Dad.'

He didn't press for an explanation, and they were half way home before Lacey said, 'The Clinton's not doing just fine, is it, Dad?' She didn't look at him, but she heard the tiny sound he made, and her hands clenched on the steering-wheel. 'The hotel's not losing money, but it isn't making much, either. Our special packages aren't being used, our ads aren't picking up much business—occupancy is down all the way around. In fact, it's gone steadily downhill for the last year, ever since Damon reopened the Kendrick Kansas City.'

Bill Clinton sighed. 'You're quite right, Lacey.'

Something inside her seemed to crumble. I was hoping that I had it wrong, she thought. Instead, he had confirmed her fears.

She swallowed hard. 'Well, we'll just have to do something to bring it back,' she said with forced cheerfulness.

'You've got a free hand, Lacey. Whatever you think we should do——'

She tried to stifle the icy shiver that crept up her spine. I didn't sign on for this! she wanted to shout. Taking some of the responsibility off her father's hands was one thing, but it felt as if the weight of the stone and brick building itself had come to rest on her shoulders.

The street in front of the Hyde Park house was jammed with parked vehicles. Where had they all come from? she wondered as she carefully threaded her brand-new little car through the maze and into the driveway.

Then she saw the banner hung across the full width of the house. 'Welcome home, Lacey', it proclaimed in letters a foot tall.

No wonder, she thought, that her mother had been so careful to make sure she would be at home tonight. No wonder her father had caught a ride with her. No doubt he had also been prepared to delay her arrival, if necessary, until it was safe...

And of all the nights for a surprise party, she thought, this must be the worst.

CHAPTER TWO

THE BIG old frame house had never been so full of people—Lacey's high school and college chums, Bill Clinton's business acquaintances, Ginny's friends from her garden clubs and bridge foursomes. There were no actual relatives, but there were several sets of Lacey's adopted aunts and uncles—people like George and Elinor Tanner, who had been Bill and Ginny's best friends for decades.

'Mother said you two were coming to dinner,' Lacey told them as they both tried to hug her at the same instant. 'She didn't tell me you were bringing along the circus and the brass band!'

'We had to do something special,' George boomed. 'We'd given up on you—we didn't think you'd ever remember the folks back home once you got to New York City.' He gave the name a sort of cowboy twang, and Lacey laughed and shook a teasing finger at him.

'You're a fine one to talk,' she accused. 'You're the guy who bought the condominium in Arizona so you would never have to shovel snow again.'

'That's different,' George said. 'Kansas City's still our home.'

'Mine, too,' Lacey reminded, and threw her arms around him. 'And I'm not going to run off because it gets cold. Oh, Uncle George, it's good to see you!'

But even so she was a little surprised to find sentimental tears in her eyes, and she laughed at herself and dashed them away and turned to greet the others who were there to welcome her home, many of whom she hadn't seen in years. Others were new faces, or almost-new ones; Grant Collins brought her a tulip glass full of a gently hissing liquid and said, 'Sorry—I couldn't find any coffee, so we'll have to start with champagne, after all.'

'That's all right,' she told him demurely. 'As long as you don't talk about my eyes.'

He looked around with a shrug. 'Whispering sweet nothings in this crowd would be a sheer waste of time.'

'I like a man who's practical,' she murmured.

He grinned at her. 'But just give me a chance, and enough quiet to fill a teaspoon——'

'I wasn't kidding about wanting to talk business,' she said. 'I'd really like to ask you a few questions.'

Grant sighed. 'Certainly, my dear. Anything you'd like to know. But let's save that for tomorrow, shall we?' He drew her off into a roomful of people.

Julia Patterson greeted her with a laugh. 'It was all I could do to stay quiet about this today,' she said.

The man standing next to her shifted the weight of a wide-eyed baby so he could put one arm awkwardly around Lacey. 'Welcome home, Lacey,' he said, and kissed her cheek.

Julia reached for the baby. 'Oh, give Lacey a proper hug, David,' she scolded. 'You haven't seen her since our wedding.'

'And I'm still heartbroken that you didn't wait for me, David,' Lacey accused, and everyone within hearing distance laughed. Lacey was grateful that they took it that way; fortunately, she thought, they all believed that the huskiness in her voice was entirely assumed. The hoarse note had startled Lacey herself; she hadn't intended to be quite that theatrical. I'll just have to be more careful, she told herself. She would never have believed that the reminder of David and Julia's wedding could still have the power to catch her by the throat.

Though to be perfectly honest, she admitted, it wasn't her memories of the wedding that were the problem. It had been a beautiful wedding on a perfect evening in June two years before, with a gloriously decorated church and a huge crowd of well-wishers, and a lavish reception afterwards at the Kendrick Kansas City...

No, it wasn't the reminder of the Pattersons' wedding that brought that painful lump to her throat, but the searing memories of the aftermath, when every ounce of pride she possessed had been stripped ruthlessly away...

And your throat only hurts tonight because you're still angry about being treated that way, she told herself, and because it's still painful to recall what a naïve and foolish child you were that night.

She stroked the baby's cheek with a gentle finger. 'Aren't you a darling?' she murmured. 'She's precious, Julia. But you didn't say anything about her today——'

'Single-mindedness,' David murmured. 'Julia can't think of more than one thing at a time. Lacey, remember the way you had to chase her wedding bouquet all over the church and the Kendrick because she would set it down to do something and then forget where she'd left it?'

'Yes—it took all eight of us bridesmaids to keep track of it.'

Julia gave a little crow of laughter. 'I'd forgotten,' she said. 'Oh, that was a wonderful day, wasn't it?'

The lump in Lacey's throat abruptly doubled in size. She nodded, and moved on. Suddenly she realised that the nagging headache she'd picked up that afternoon had increased to a violent throbbing that felt as if jungle drums were pounding inside her head. The volume of noise throughout the house wasn't helping matters, either.

'What's wrong?' Grant asked softly. 'You look miserable.'

She shook her head in denial. What good could it possibly do to admit to being in pain? It would only spoil her parents' pleasure in their party. They were so outrageously pleased at having managed to surprise her.

Just then one of her father's golf partners lost control of his glass while describing a putt he'd missed that afternoon, and Scotch and soda cascaded down the front of Lacey's suit. She stopped and closed her eyes for a second in sheer agony before she could paste a smile on her face again. 'It's quite all right,' she said. 'I wanted to change clothes, anyway. After all, everyone here had the advantage of me—at least you knew you were coming to a party!' It was true enough, she thought, and it was a relief to have an excuse to escape for a few minutes, even at the cost of her favourite suit.

Her mother was supervising the caterer's men as they set up a dinner buffet in the dining-room. 'Move that tray another six inches to the left,' she directed, and then smiled brightly at Lacey. 'I saw your face when you got out of the car,' she said. 'It truly was a surprise, wasn't it?'

Shock was more like it, Lacey thought. 'You could say that.' She snatched a boiled shrimp off a parsley-trimmed centrepiece, and earned a frown from the caterer.

'Goodness, darling, you smell like a distillery,' Ginny said, wrinkling her nose.

Lacey told her about the missed putt. 'The water hazards at the country club have nothing on him,' she said. 'He's a Scotch and soda hazard. I'm going to sneak up the back stairs and change.'

'Don't be long, dear. There are a hundred people who want to see you.' Ginny turned back to the caterer.

'That's what I was afraid of,' Lacey muttered. She waited till she was out of sight to make a face. It helped a little.

Her own room felt like a haven, a citadel to be defended to the death against the raging mobs outside. She swallowed two aspirin tablets and put a cold cloth across her face for a couple of minutes. But she knew if she stayed much longer her mother would come looking for her, and then she'd have to explain why she was hiding in her room. So she tossed the stained suit over the back of a chair, put on a yellow-green sundress instead, and went back downstairs.

And walked straight into Damon Kendrick at the front door.

Of course, she thought. Dad could hardly avoid inviting Damon, when he'd asked everyone else in the hotel business in this town to come to her party. But why did the man actually have to come?

The answer was instantaneous and obvious. Because it didn't matter a damn to him, she realised. If he remembered that night two years ago at all, it was probably with amusement at the memory of a girl so naïve that she'd actually believed Damon Kendrick would want to marry her.

Lacey gave herself a mental shake. Well, that inexperienced girl had grown up enough to know that she wasn't going to embarrass herself again, she resolved. And so she stepped forward and offered her hand, and smiled at him. 'Thanks for coming,' she said, and her voice was almost normal.

It was the woman next to him who answered. 'Our pleasure,' she said, and her silver fingernails closed possessively on Damon's sleeve. She was a platinum blonde—the variety that came out of a bottle, Lacey would bet her last dollar.

And, she thought spitefully, she probably calls herself Candy or Lulu or Bambi, or something equally sexist and demeaning. She looks that type. Just the kind Damon Kendrick would find intriguing—for a short while, at least.

And to think, she told herself viciously, that once he thought I belonged in that category, too. Now I really have a headache...

The party showed no signs of winding down early. Lacey stayed as far as she could from Damon and the lady of the silver nails without being obvious about it. It wasn't hard; within a few minutes he'd gravitated towards her father's den at the back of the house, where a cut-throat poker game had already begun, and the lady, doing a good imitation of a puppy on a leash, had followed. Lacey made it a point to stay at the other end of the house, but she didn't forget that he was there. At any moment, she reminded herself, he might get on to a losing streak and decide to seek out other amusement.

So she stayed watchful, while she laughed and danced and ate and drank, occasionally stopping to explain an old memory to Grant, who seemed to be attached to her elbow with an invisible string. She was glad of that to-night; so many of her old friends had paired off now, and it was pleasant not to be entirely alone.

And finally the party was over. With the buffet table ravaged and the bar closed, a few of the older set collapsed in the living-room, while some of the younger ones urged Lacey to come with them to Westport, just to see what was going on in the nightspots there. She shook her still aching head, and cheerfully said her goodbyes at the front door.

Grant was last in line. He took her hands and said, 'If all your old friends can kiss you goodbye, then surely I can, as well.' And before she could feel more than a whisper of panic at the confident assumption in his voice, he had slipped an arm around her and drawn her close. It must have looked like quite a casual kiss, much like the others she had received that night, but it held a suggestion of permanence, as if Grant was certain this was only the first.

Then he squeezed her hand and smiled at her and said, 'We have a date for tomorrow, so I can answer all your questions about the hotel. I'll do my homework tonight.'

She protested. 'Actually, it's only general information I need, Grant.'

He smiled down into her eyes. 'No company secret is too sacred to share with you, my dear. And I don't think I could sleep anyway, for thinking about you.' It was a husky promise, and then he was gone.

Lacey braced herself against the carved newel post and closed her eyes in pain. Did I really encourage him to think that way? she asked herself in momentary panic. I only met the man this afternoon!

'Congratulate me, Lacey,' George Tanner said in his booming voice, a little subdued now by the cigar stub he was clenching between his teeth. 'I actually finished the evening a winner.'

Feeling distinctly uneasy, Lacey turned to face the men who had been back in the den, playing poker.

'Don't rub it in, George,' Bill Clinton said, and added philosophically, 'We can't all be winners, can we, Damon?'

Damon's gaze slid over Lacey. What did he see? she wondered. Dishevelled hair? Lipstick missing, where it had been kissed away?

Don't be silly, she told herself tartly. You sound as if you think he might be jealous—as if you'd like him to be jealous—when there's nothing further from the truth!

He turned his head a fraction and looked woodenly at the front door, and then Lacey knew that he hadn't seen just the evidence of that last warm kiss, but the act itself. And had he perhaps heard what Grant had said, about passing along company secrets? Grant had been only teasing, she was sure, but would Damon know that?

Grant, you're a fool, she thought. You may have sacrificed your job with that remark tonight...

And, if he had, she was at least partly responsible, and she owed it to Grant to try to straighten it out, she told herself.

The lady of the silver fingernails came down the hall from the powder-room and attached herself once more to Damon's arm. They were moving towards the door when Lacey stepped forward and said, 'Damon!'

It came out more sharply than she had intended, like a demand issued by a petulant female. The lady at Damon's side raised her well-plucked eyebrows as if she recognised the tone of voice. Even Bill Clinton looked a little startled, and Lacey felt herself colour in embarrassment—but there was nothing she could do except go on. She took two steps towards Damon. 'I need to talk to you.'

He looked her over thoughtfully. 'Not right now, surely?' he said. 'It's late.' The platinum blonde beside him giggled.

I think I am going to be sick, Lacey thought. She bit her lip, and said, trying to sound reasonable, 'Why not now? It will only take a minute. I just want your permission to talk to Grant about some of the Kendrick's promotional ideas, and the renovation, and some things I'm thinking of trying at the Clinton.'

He didn't say anything for a long moment, but he looked as if he was turning all the possibilities over in his head.

The lack of reaction piqued her. 'It's nothing that would violate your corporate security, let me assure you,' she added tartly. 'As far as that goes, I could spy and find out what you're offering, but I'd much rather do it openly—'

'Why ask Grant?'

'Why?' It surprised her. 'Because I want to know, that's why! He's the general manager, for heaven's sake!'

'If you're interested in the renovation, perhaps I should tell you that Grant wasn't there when it was done.'

'I know. Still, I'm sure he can answer any questions——'

He interrupted smoothly. 'So can I, Lacey. Probably better. Why not ask me?'

The silence stretched out into aeons. Lacey was uneasily aware of the audience in the hallway. This wasn't too smart, she thought. I should have phoned him tomorrow——

She swallowed twice, convulsively. 'I assumed you'd be too busy. And Grant offered.'

'I gathered that.'

'But of course I'd rather have your help, Damon.' She was proud of herself; her voice didn't even tremble.

He looked her over for a long moment. 'I can see you at seven o'clock tomorrow morning, at the Kendrick,' he said crisply.

She eyed the platinum blonde. She looks a bit disappointed, Lacey thought caustically, as if she'd hoped to keep him in bed a little longer than that. 'Are you certain that isn't too early, Damon?'

'Why?' he asked softly. 'Are you expecting to be hung over?'

'Of course not!'

'That's the only time I can spare. Will you be there, or not?'

He had thrown down a challenge, and Lacey knew that if she walked away from it she could never forgive herself.

She met his eyes steadily. 'Seven o'clock,' she said. 'I'll be there.'

At five minutes to seven the next morning the entire sixteenth floor of the Kendrick Kansas City was dark. Not even a cleaning lady broke the hushed silence behind the tightly locked glass doors that closed the headquarters of Hoteliers, Inc. away from the rest of the hotel. There was not a secretary in evidence, not a receptionist, and certainly not the chairman of the board.

Lacey's first reaction was almost cynical amusement. So the lady of the silver fingernails had won, after all, she thought. Then the irritable suspicion that he had never intended to keep the appointment took root, and grew to anger. Surely, if he was in the habit of early-morning meetings, there would be someone on duty to answer the telephone, turn on the lights and make coffee?

She stormed back downstairs. The lobby was quiet at this hour, with only a few business customers checking out at the desk. The elderly man at the assistant manager's desk looked up with a smile.

'I am supposed to meet Mr Kendrick this morning,' Lacey began. 'But——'

His brow wrinkled a little. 'You're Miss Clinton?'

She was startled. 'Yes. How——'

He snapped his fingers at a bellboy. 'Mr Kendrick asked that you come upstairs. Jack will take you up.' He passed a key across the desk to the young man.

'I've *been* upstairs,' Lacey pointed out. 'There's no one in the Hoteliers office at all——'

'This way, miss,' the bellboy said, and Lacey subsided with a sigh. Damon must have left those instructions last night, before the platinum blonde had got all his attention. They would soon find out that there had been a mistake.

The bellboy led her to a small alcove in the corner of the lobby, half-hidden behind a marble pillar, and used the key to summon a tiny wood-panelled elevator, just big enough for two people and a narrow, padded bench. It startled Lacey. On the wall were just two buttons.

Up and down, that's a safe assumption, she told herself, with a half-hysterical giggle.

The elevator itself was obviously old, salvaged from the renovation, but it ran as smoothly and quietly as the most modern technology could boast. She glanced at herself in the bevelled mirror on one wall and tried surreptitiously to smooth away the lines around her eyes. She hadn't slept at all, and though, thank heaven, her headache was gone, and she had a nasty feeling that there might be another lurking just around the corner.

The elevator whooshed to a stop. Lacey stepped out and then halted in mid-step in the centre of the little lobby. 'This isn't the——' she began, and then bit her tongue, hard. So Damon was going to have his pound of flesh, was he? Well, he would find that she wasn't so easily humiliated as she had been two years ago. Besides, there was no sense in letting the bellboy share the man's little joke. She knew from long experience how efficiently hotel grapevines worked.

So she stood there in silence and let him knock on the walnut door that so obviously led not to Damon Kendrick's office, but to his apartment, or penthouse suite, or whatever he called it. And when the door swung open she took a deep breath and stepped across the threshold.

Damon propped an arm against the door and looked down at her. 'You're late,' he said.

'I assumed, when you said "at the Kendrick", that you meant your office. You certainly didn't say anything about coming to your apartment——'

'I thought you would prefer not to give anyone ideas. There were several people listening in last night when we set up this little rendezvous, you know.'

'This is not a rendezvous. This is a business conference, and I'd like to carry on in a businesslike way. Preferably in your office——'

'You're sounding like a prude, Lacey.'

'I'm so sorry if it offends you.'

'I can't say it surprises me, that's sure. I should have suspected from the beginning that your views would be just as old-fashioned as your name is.'

'It's a perfectly good family name, and it has nothing to do with my moral code.'

'Whatever you say.' The corner of his mouth quirked humorously. 'In any case, if you're expecting Bree to pop out of a closet somewhere and embarrass you, don't worry. She isn't here.'

'Bree,' Lacey said. 'Of course. She would have a name like that. Actually, I assumed when you had me dragged up here that you had made sure the coast was clear, but——'

'Dragged? Don't you mean escorted, Lacey? I'm only being polite, you know. I've moved since the last time you visited my home. Not that you ever came there often—it would have been too dangerous to your reputation, I suppose. It was much safer for you to stay in public, where I couldn't very well act as I'd have liked——'

Her chest hurt a little at the reminder of the few times when she had gone to his apartment, and dreamed of the day when it would be their first home, together . . . 'Is that why you insisted on bringing me up here today? So your employees can speculate about what we're doing?'

His voice was level. 'Not at all. What interest do I have in your reputation?'

None, she thought. But then, you never did, Damon. You would have ruined me in a minute to suit your own selfish interests. Not that you would have regarded it in that light, of course—you probably would have thought you were doing me a favour...

'You did say something about business,' he reminded. 'Actually, I had them bring you up here so we could have breakfast while we talked.'

'I'm flattered.'

'Don't be. I refuse to skip meals, even for the pleasure of your company, and I cannot stand an office that smells of bacon and eggs.' He smiled suddenly, and there was in his eyes a trace of the charm that had so nearly been her undoing two years before. 'Come on, Lacey, before I start gnawing the carpets,' he cajoled lightly, and led her through the spacious living-room and into a compact dining-room that looked south over the city.

Lacey shot one look at the silent-footed man who was lifting covers from the service plates already arranged on the polished table, and walked across to the wide windows.

The sun was already brilliant—it would be another warm day—but it was still low enough to cast long and fantastic shadows across the landscape and form a sort of crazy quilt out of the multitude of architectural styles and colours and designs that made up Kansas City.

'It's beautiful,' she said. 'I see why you wanted this. This was one of the imperial suites before, wasn't it?'

'Both of them, actually. And it seemed to be more sensible to use the space myself than to have the suites standing empty more than half the time.'

'There's a flaw in that reasoning,' Lacey decided.

Damon smiled. 'Well, yes, there is. Actually, I decided there should be a perk here and there for being in my position.'

'I'd say this qualifies as a major one.' She picked out a landmark or two on the horizon. It must be gorgeous up here at night, she thought.

'Thank you, Humphrey,' he said softly. 'That will be all.'

The delicate smell of Canadian bacon drew her over to the table. Damon held her chair and then seated himself across from her. Lacey held her fork poised for a moment over the golden-brown omelette, admiring the picture it made on the china plate, and then cut into it. Cheese, mushrooms and bits of green pepper oozed gently on to her plate.

'Normally I don't eat much for breakfast, but Humphrey should get a medal for producing this,' she said contentedly. 'Is he your butler, or valet, or what?'

'He refers to himself as a gentleman's gentleman.'

She raised innocent eyes to his. 'Well, he's half right,' she conceded.

'That was a cheap shot, Lacey.'

She knew it, and she was almost ashamed of herself.

'Are you thinking of renovating the Clinton?'

It was an idle, careless question, and Lacey's instincts instantly warned her to be careful. 'If I were, would I tell you first?' she countered. 'After all, you're my strongest competitor.'

'You're the one who wanted this conference,' he pointed out lazily. 'I can't very well answer your questions if I don't know what they are—and you mentioned the Kendrick's renovation yourself last night.'

She bit her lip, and drew a line in the cheese sauce on her plate with the tine of her fork.

'Shall we stop fencing and just talk?' Damon said. 'If it will make you feel better, I suggest that we treat this conference as an off-the-record event, and that we both cross our hearts and promise not to take commercial advantage of anything that is said here.'

'All right,' she said slowly. But she didn't quite know how to go on.

'The alternative to an honest talk,' he said blandly, 'is that I'm going to think the whole thing was a put-up job because you wanted the pleasure of looking at me.'

She gave him a venomous stare.

'If it makes you feel better, I don't consider the Clinton to be much competition these days, Lacey.'

She thought that one over, and said, 'I see. Of course, I already suspected that you were taking our clients away.'

'We get a good number of them. Does that mean you're going to try to put up a fight to get them back?'

She bristled. 'Of course I am. You make it sound like a hopeless job.' She put her fork down and stared across the table at him. 'You really think it's impossible, don't you?'

He didn't answer directly. 'I suggested to your father two years ago that he take his chances with us and make the investment to turn the Clinton into a first-class hotel again. But he couldn't see what was coming, and now he's paying the price. The Clinton is on a slide that it won't come out of unless someone spends the money to make it a modern hotel.'

'Oh, I'm not dumb, Damon,' she said crossly. 'I know we've got to redecorate, do some sprucing up——'

'More than that, Lacey. Your physical plant is run down. You've got antiquated plumbing and heating and electrical systems. You've got rooms that were considered huge and luxurious sixty years ago, but which look like telephone booths to today's traveller. You've got bathrooms that are about as modern as dinosaurs, and——'

'I see I'm not the only one who thought of using spies to see what the competition was up to,' she said coolly.

'I wouldn't call it spying. Spend a night in one of your own rooms, and you'll see what I mean. The real problem is, as soon as you put a crowbar into that hotel to make an improvement, you've got the whole mess to handle at once. It needs to be closed down and rebuilt from scratch. Just putting up new draperies and wallpaper isn't going to do it.'

She set her cup down with a firm little click against the china saucer, and said sweetly, 'You'd love to see it closed, wouldn't you, Damon Kendrick?'

'I certainly would,' he admitted.

'That way you'd get the rest of our clients——'

'Possibly. But in a year or two, when it reopened, we'd both be making money from it. I don't have enough rooms here for a big convention, and neither do you. But together——'

'I'm surprised you haven't just bought it, then.'

'Bill didn't want to sell. He seemed to think he should keep it in the family, for you.'

'Poor Damon,' she cooed. 'If you'd only been able to bring yourself to marry me, you wouldn't have had this problem.'

'There are certain things that aren't worth the cost, Lacey.'

It hurt, worse than anything had in the two years that had passed since the first time he had told her that—the first time, she thought, that he had ever been completely honest with her. 'How lucky I am that you have a few scruples,' she said tightly. 'And, of course, that you didn't want me so badly after all.'

'I never said I didn't want you,' he pointed out silkily.

She pushed a bite of her omelette around on the plate. It no longer looked so tasty. 'As long as we're talking in hypothetical terms,' she challenged, 'just how much would this total renovation cost, do you think? Or didn't your spies get that far?'

He didn't rise to the bait. 'Off the top of my head, I'd guess six to ten million dollars if you did it on the cheap,' he said promptly. 'Anywhere from fifteen on up if you do it right.'

She felt a little faint.

Damon pushed his plate aside and refilled her coffee-cup. 'Bill can raise the money,' he said. 'The value is there, though it might be a challenge to find a banker with enough vision to see the possibilities. The real question is, does he want to? He's sixty years old—that's a big risk to take at his age. And every dollar he's got is tied up in that hotel.'

'It's always been his life.'

Damon nodded. 'I know that, Lacey. He's from the old school. But an independent hotel has a hard time of it these days, and it's going to get nothing but tougher. Your competition isn't me, you know—not any more. It's every chain that puts up a pre-fabricated building on the outskirts of town and advertises a budget rate. Unless you make the Clinton a first-class hotel again——'

He didn't have to finish the sentence. Lacey knew what he meant. The alternative was for the Clinton to keep wearing down and tiring out, until finally it became nothing more than a shelter for the city's poverty-stricken, because no one else wanted to stay there.

She shook herself. That's ridiculous, she thought. He's painted a picture that's horrifyingly realistic, but that doesn't make it the truth. It's to his advantage to make you think twice about the future, and then sell him the place for a bargain price!

'To say nothing of the constant attention it takes, and the energy a job like that absorbs,' Damon went on. 'How long is Bill going to be willing to give sixteen hours a day to the hotel? Or is he going to turn it over to you?'

'Eventually.'

'You've been gone two years, right? A little more than that, actually—it was June, wasn't it?'

'Do you expect me to be flattered that you remember?'

He didn't answer. 'Were you working in hotels while you were gone?'

'No,' she admitted.

'I didn't think so.' Or you wouldn't be asking such idiotic questions, he seemed to be thinking.

'I can learn,' she flared.

'But can you learn in time?'

She didn't have an answer for that. Before she could think of one, he pushed his monogrammed cuff up and checked the heavy gold watch on his wrist. 'Any other questions?'

She shook her head, absently.

'I've asked Grant to show you though the Kendrick this morning. I think it will help you see the magnitude of the problem you're facing.' He pushed his chair back. 'He should be here any minute.'

'Here? You told him I'd be here?'

His eyebrows arched. 'Would you rather I'd kept it secret, and made it appear there was something to hide? I could sneak you down the elevator and out the back door, I suppose, but——'

'Oh, never mind. I wouldn't expect you to understand, anyway.' She jumped up from the table and threw her napkin down.

'I'm sure you can explain it to him. All it would take are a few of those soft, enticing kisses of yours. Kisses that promise him anything... Are you delivering on those promises these days, Lacey, or still just leading people on?'

She spun around. 'Why, you—I never led you on! I absolutely never——'

'Oh?' he said drily. 'And I suppose you're going to say you never implied that you found me sexually ex-

citing, either, or insinuated that you were eager to find
out what I was like in bed——?'

'I——' She stopped, and then turned her back on him
and stared, unseeing, out of the wide window. I can
hardly tell him that, she thought, when he was the most
sexually exciting male I'd ever run across.

And as for sleeping with him—well, when she had
thought that he loved her, she'd been dying to sleep with
him, and only the thought of a perfect wedding night
had held her back. And after he'd told her the truth,
and she had understood that he didn't know the meaning
of love, that his feeling for her had been no more than
the lust he felt for women like the platinum blonde with
the silver fingernails——

Bree, she thought in disgust. What in the hell kind of
woman lets herself be diminished like that?

She shivered a little, and Damon spoke from just
behind her, so close that his breath stirred the soft red
hair at her temple.

'Nervous?' he asked solicitously. 'We are almost alone
up here, you know, and Humphrey has very convenient
lapses of hearing.'

'I'm sure he does,' she snapped. 'And of course I'm
not nervous. I know I'm perfectly safe here. You only
want to get a reaction, to soothe your bruised pride. You
couldn't possibly want to—to——'

'To make love to you? You're quite wrong, you know.
Because I would be very willing to satisfy your curiosity——'

'I am not curious about what you like to do in bed!'

He turned her gently towards him, and stroked a gentle
finger across her bottom lip. 'Aren't you?' he said softly,
and his mouth came down on hers.

CHAPTER THREE

IT TOOK every sliver of courage and self-control she possessed to stand there quietly and let him kiss her, when she wanted to scream, to kick him, to batter her fists against his face until he had to let her go. But it would be far more effective, she knew, to simply stand there unmoved and let him kiss her, and then, when he was finished, to walk away coldly and show him that it hadn't mattered at all.

His mouth was gentle, mobile, unhurried. He didn't demand or plead; he simply caressed her as calmly as if he had the right to do so, as if he'd been kissing her like that every day of her life, and was confident that she liked it.

As I did once, she thought, a little dizzily. How much I liked it! When I believed that I loved him, I used to collect the memory of kisses like this, and I held them close to me when I went to sleep at night so I could dream of him.

The tip of his tongue teased gently between her lips and lingered there, as if he was savouring the taste of her. The doorbell chimed discreetly, and at the same instant she made a half-conscious little sound, a sort of combination protest and moan of pleasure.

'Don't fret,' he muttered against her mouth. 'Humphrey will answer that, and Grant can kick his heels for the whole morning for all I care. We won't be interrupted——'

'What a pity!' she gasped, and with the last fragment of her strength she pulled herself out of his arms and turned her back on him, one fist pressed against her mouth, trying desperately to get herself under control again.

'I suppose you're going to tell me that you didn't enjoy that?' he said quietly. He sounded as if he wasn't breathing quite right himself.

'I didn't. Not in the least.'

He pulled her back against him with a jerk till her spine was pressed against his chest. His hands slid over her shoulders, coming to rest just where the swell of her breasts began, the fingertips seeking the delicate hollow at the base of her throat where a hammering pulse betrayed her.

'The hell you didn't,' he muttered, and his hands slipped down to cup her breasts. The thin fabric of her blouse seemed to burn away under his touch.

She put her right elbow into the vulnerable spot just beneath his ribs with all the force she could muster, and was fiercely glad to hear his startled, painful gasp.

'In the future,' she said icily, 'please keep your hands off me, Damon.' She didn't look at him as she turned on her heel and went to greet Grant, who jumped up from a couch in the big living-room. Today, as he had yesterday, he was wearing the pale blue jacket that marked a member of the staff of the Kendrick Kansas City, with an engraved name-tag on the breast pocket.

'Good morning,' he told her, but he didn't quite look her in the eye.

'Lacey would like the whole tour,' Damon said smoothly, behind her. 'Show her anything she likes—answer any questions she may have.'

Grant shot a look at him. He looked surprised. 'Of course.' He reached for the door-handle. 'Where shall we start, Lacey?'

'I'd like to see some of the remodelled rooms, please.'

'Certainly. Grant?' Damon added smoothly. He was leaning against the arched doorway that divided the living-room from the small entrance foyer. He hadn't put on his jacket yet, and he looked at ease, comfortable, unhurried. 'Thanks for waiting around till we finished with—breakfast.' It was perfectly cordial and innocuous, and yet there was just enough tactful hesitation before the final word to suggest that they had been involved in any activities the listener cared to infer, but that they had certainly not been merely having breakfast; it made Lacey want to strangle him right there.

She held her head high and walked out of the apartment without another word. She could feel Grant watching her in the tiny elevator, and it took stern self-control to keep from checking the mirror to make sure she was still all in one piece.

He led her across the now-bustling lobby to the main bank of elevators and pushed a button for one of the upper floors. 'Sorry about the indirect route we're taking,' he said, 'but it's necessary. Mr Kendrick insists on his privacy, so it's impossible to get off his elevator on any other floor.'

It was matter-of-fact, the employee simply making a statement about his employer, without implying any judgement at all. In those few moments in the foyer of Damon's penthouse, Lacey thought, the friendly companion of last night, the man who had kissed her goodnight as if he'd like to do it regularly, had vanished. Grant had retired into a businesslike manner, as quickly as a tortoise could retreat into his shell.

Perhaps, she thought, I underestimated his own sense of self-preservation last night. He obviously is going to take no chances around someone who can get Damon Kendrick's attention at this hour of the morning, for breakfast and—other things, she told herself tartly. What

Grant believed they'd been doing might as well be written on his forehead in neon lights.

And there wasn't much sense in trying to explain it away, Lacey told herself. After all, even though she hadn't invited that sort of behaviour from Damon, she had been quite thoroughly kissed. And, even if she could honestly deny it, why should she bother?

I only met Grant yesterday, she thought irritably. Why on earth should I have to explain anything to him, anyway?

'I'm amazed he didn't arrange his elevator to stop at the corporate floor, at least,' she said stiffly. 'That way he wouldn't have to mix with the riff-raff at all.'

He looked surprised at the tone of her voice.

She gritted her teeth and turned the conversation back to business. 'Are all the Kendrick's rooms alike now?'

'Oh, no. That would have been impossible, considering the original floor plan. And in any case, why would we want it to look like the assembly-line manufactured units?' He tapped perfunctorily on a door before using a credit-card shaped key to unlock it, and then propped the panel open.

Very smart, Lacey thought. Keeping the door open is a very intelligent and unobtrusive way to protect himself—not from me, I hope, but from Damon. Yes, I underestimated Grant, all right; that's probably why he's managed to survive in this job longer than his predecessors have . . .

'The old Kendrick had nearly twice the number of rooms as we have now,' he said. 'The old ones were cramped and high-ceilinged—hard to heat, hard to clean, not very comfortable for guests. By making two rooms into one, we ended up with spacious elegant quarters, well-proportioned rooms, plenty of cupboard space, light, air——'

He sounds like a salesman, Lacey thought. But he was right—it was a very pleasant room, inviting and restful with its plum-coloured carpet and soft pastel walls. She peeped through a door into a gleaming white bathroom, and raised her eyebrows when she found a second one at the other end of the room.

Grant nodded. 'A good many of the rooms have two baths, which is a real luxury for families. That's the thing that gets the most favourable comments on our survey cards. Finished?'

She nodded. As they walked down the hall, he pointed out the architectural changes that had allowed space for all the new modifications. 'It looks pretty minor, really,' he said, and Lacey nodded. She wouldn't have seen them herself. 'Mr Kendrick insisted that the atmosphere of the hotel not be violated by the changes. But I understand it gave the architects headaches for months. We have an entirely new sprinkler system, too, and new fire doors and fire escapes—we far exceed what the city code requires. Mr Kendrick made sure of that.'

'Probably only because he lives here, too. Please don't try to make him out to be a hero just to please me, Grant,' Lacey said drily.

Then she regretted it, because for the next hour Grant said nothing much at all as he showed her over the rest of the building. He answered her questions, of course, tersely and directly to the point, but that was the only time he had a comment.

By the time they had toured the entire hotel—including the sub-basements and the kitchens and the elevator shafts—and reached the lobby again, Lacey couldn't wait to get out of the place. She'd seen so much that it would take days just to remember it all—and longer yet, she thought, to sort it out.

'Well,' Grant said hesitantly, 'if you have any more questions——'

'I will have, I'm sure, but just now I can't even think.'

'Would you like some coffee? Or breakfast?' It was a half-hearted offer, she thought.

'I've had breakfast, thanks,' she said icily. 'Remember?'

'I thought——' Grant stumbled to a halt and flushed scarlet. Even the lobes of his ears turned red. 'Sorry,' he said miserably, and suddenly it was very important to her that this misunderstanding of his be straightened out.

'I know what you thought. It was precisely what Damon intended you to think.' She saw a trace of doubt in his eyes, and said tartly, 'Oh, for heaven's sake, Grant, ask your own staff what time I arrived this morning. They'll tell you I wasn't up there long enough to be mauled——'

Not much, at any rate, she told her own prickly conscience. Not enough to matter.

'You didn't get here till this morning?'

'Did you actually think I'd been up there all night?'

He looked thoroughly ashamed of himself. 'Mr Kendrick called me last night, you see, to ask if I'd give you the tour this morning. It was more than two hours after I left the party, so I thought surely——'

'That I must be with him,' she whispered. 'The damned, cunning devil——'

'It was just business, then, this morning?'

'Did you really think it could be anything else?'

'When it comes to him,' Grant said with a trace of cynicism, 'nobody ever knows quite what to think. Now, shall we have that coffee, after all?'

Lacey found herself thinking late that afternoon, as she sipped yet another cup of stale coffee in her office at the Clinton, that Grant's comment should be the epitaph carved into Damon Kendrick's tombstone when the time came. 'Nobody ever knew what to think of him,' she quoted drily to herself. Certainly, she hadn't, even though she had believed that she knew him so very, very well...

She had always known who he was, of course; a young woman with any connection with the hotel business in Kansas City could hardly escape knowing about the man who had, when he was ridiculously young, taken over the Kendrick empire after the untimely death of his father in a shooting accident, and within two years doubled its size and profits.

But, from the first day she had actually met Damon Kendrick in her father's office, it had not been the power he wielded or the wealth he controlled that drew her, but the sheer magnetism of the man himself, tall and lean and dark, and stunningly good-looking.

When the opportunity came, and she was seated beside him at a banquet to raise money for one of the multitude of charities that Ginny worked for, Lacey had taken advantage of it. She had flirted with him throughout dinner, feeling all the time as if she was walking a tightrope without a net and that one mis-step would doom her hopes...

That's odd, she mused. I didn't realise till now that even on that very first night I had my plans made.

He'd been pleasant enough that evening, but she had gone home afterwards with an utterly sick emptiness in her chest. What, after all, could a man like Damon Kendrick possibly see in her? And as the days went on she came to believe that all her careful balancing act had been in vain, and that he'd only been being polite to the daughter of a colleague...

She smiled a little, a tender, nostalgic smile, as she remembered the evening a couple of weeks after that banquet, when her father had answered the telephone and then said, 'Yes, Damon, what can I do for you?'

An instant later he had turned to her to say, in a voice that creaked with surprise, 'It's Damon Kendrick, and he wants to talk to you, Lacey! Why would Damon Kendrick want——'

She had seized the telephone before he could finish the question. Lacey knew her father had all the respect in the world for Damon as a competitor. And while Bill Clinton had taken every one of her male friends in stride over the years, no matter what their oddities, she wasn't about to give him an opportunity to object to the prospect of Damon Kendrick as his daughter's boyfriend. Damon was different.

Boyfriend. She smiled, remembering. What an absurd term to attach to him! He'd been thirty-one then, and all of Lacey's college friends had looked like callow fools, interested only in cheerleaders and beer parties, next to this mature man who controlled a network of hotels that stretched across North America...

That was where she had made her mistake, perhaps, she thought. Because Damon was so serious about his business, she had assumed he felt that way about his personal life as well. And, though he had never mentioned marriage, still she knew, as winter wore on into spring and she saw him more and more often, that it was only a matter of time. Because it was obvious that they were very compatible. They liked each other as well as loving, and as for the rest—well, whenever he kissed her she knew that happiness lay within her grasp, and if she was patient she would have the whole of her life to share that perfect bliss with him. In the meantime, there was college to finish, and Julia's wedding coming up——

The only blot on Lacey's landscape that spring, if indeed there had been one at all, was the fact that Julia's parents were holding her wedding reception at the Kendrick, instead of the Clinton. It would have been a

perfect day otherwise, Lacey thought. A glorious, sparkling June wedding day that cooled into a perfect
evening...

She had dreamed of her own wedding so often that
being a part of Julia's was almost second nature. She
was the calm one who kept everyone on course, rescuing
Julia's bouquet from the odd places she left it, and re-
hemming a dress with cellophane tape after a careless
high heel had ripped the stitches out.

But her own dreams were never far beneath the
surface. As she drifted down the long, ribbon-draped
aisle in her ice-blue bridesmaid's dress, she could almost
feel the weight of a long ivory satin train tugging at her.
She could almost feel the smooth dark sleeve of her
father's jacket under her lace-gloved hand. And she
could almost see the love in Damon's eyes as he waited
for her at the end of the aisle...

That was where the daydream ended. David Patterson
was a nice enough sort, goodness knew; Lacey had dated
him herself for a while, and she was careful who she
associated with. But she couldn't quite understand why
Julia was so head-over-heels in love with him that she
could scarcely remember her own name. When there were
men like Damon in the world, what woman would settle
for a David?

Damon hadn't been a member of the wedding party,
but when the horse-drawn carriages had brought them
from the church to the reception he had been waiting
under the canopy at the front of the Kendrick Kansas
City. He had lifted her down from the carriage, and
whispered in her ear something wicked about how very
tantalising she looked tonight in her icicle costume, and
then he laughed at the way she had pretended to be
shocked and took her up to the Grand Ballroom, where
acres of organdie and miles of ribbon had formed a

heavenly cloud on which to dine and dance and sip champagne...

And later that evening, after a wonderful dinner which she was really too excited to eat, and after a good deal more champagne than her mother would have thought was prudent, he took her hand and they slipped out of the Grand Ballroom and into a tiny, hidden alcove nearby. That was one of the advantages of dating him, Lacey had found; he always knew where the private nooks and crannies were.

He hadn't kissed her all evening. She had always liked the fact that he never put their feelings for each other on public display, but that night she had been throbbing with desire by the time they were alone, and he knew it. His kisses had never been quite so demanding before, never quite so certain, so masterful. She had quickly been reduced to a quivering shell, every nerve vibrating under the assault on her senses.

He pressed his lips to the very edge of her low-cut bodice, where the swell of her breast rose and fell with her gasps, and said, unsteadily, 'Lacey, I want to do so much more than this.'

'I know,' she breathed. 'I know.'

He raised his head, and his dark eyes held a painful glow that she had never seen there before. 'Come upstairs with me,' he said hoarsely. 'I need to make love to you tonight, Lacey——'

On a night like this, she thought, with magic in the air, to be alone with the man she adored, and find the supreme way to express her love——

Reason raised its inconvenient head. 'What if someone comes looking for me?' she whispered miserably.

'The pictures are taken. The bride and groom are gone. No one will notice one bridesmaid more or less. Please, Lacey——'

But the madness was receding. 'Oh, darling,' she said mistily, 'don't you see? I want us to have this sort of a wedding night ourselves—when we don't have to be in a hurry because no one can come between us ever again——'

For a moment, she didn't realise what was happening; she only knew that Damon's arms were suddenly like lead weights around her. 'Wedding night,' he repeated, and his voice was absolutely expressionless.

'We'll make it a perfect night—our first one together,' she said. Apprehension was growing in her; she felt as if she was suddenly fighting a battle against an enemy she couldn't see, an enemy that had attacked her from some hidden quarter.

'I've never said anything about weddings, Lacey,' he said. He let her go then, and stood with his arms folded across his chest, his breath coming as if he'd just run a marathon. 'Never.'

'But—I assumed——'

'I see. You assumed.' He didn't sound angry, exactly, she thought, and yet something about him terrified her. 'And you've spent this whole spring leading me on a dance designed to keep me out of your bed until I did the honourable thing and married you, is that it?'

'Damon!' It was only a horrified whisper. Her throat was so dry, she couldn't have screamed.

'Well, it isn't going to work, Lacey. I won't be owned, by you or any other woman, ever. You want to go to bed with me just as much as I want you, and I'm not going to be blackmailed into giving you a wedding ring as the price for my enjoyment.'

In that instant the glorious pink cloud she had lived in all spring turned to a wet grey fog that threatened to choke her.

'It isn't personal, Lacey,' he said, more gently. 'You understand that, don't you? It's just that there will never be a Mrs Kendrick. I will take my fun where I find it, and I will not ever be tied down, to you or any other woman.'

Not personal? How can he say that? she thought. I've invested every ounce of myself in him, and he's telling me not to take this personally? 'All you wanted was a one-night stand?'

'Not necessarily,' he said. He reached out to touch a lock of her hair, almost gently. 'I think it might take quite a while to get tired of you, Lacey——'

She jerked away from his touch. 'I thought you loved me!' If she had had control of her voice, it would have been a shriek. As it was, she could only utter a sort of frenzied whisper.

'Oh, Lacey.' He looked almost sad, she thought. 'What is love, anyway? Isn't it better to be honest with each other——?'

'You could have been a little more honest with me!'

'I never said I wanted to marry you.' His voice was razor-edged, and it cut just as surely. 'You dreamed that fairy-tale up in your own little mind.'

She could no longer bear the pain, then. She had pushed aside the heavy velvet curtain that sheltered the little alcove, and stumbled down the grand staircase from the mezzanine, and fled across the lobby, where she collided with the revolving door they had come through so happily just hours before...

She pushed the cold coffee aside with an oath. 'Lacey, why must you go over it all again?' she asked. The empty office didn't answer. 'You were an idiot, that's all, and you deserved what you got. If you'd had any sense at all——'

But she hadn't, and so everything had gone awry. She had fled not only the hotel, but, within a few weeks, the city. She had not told her parents the details. The bare facts had hurt them badly enough; both of them had come to love Damon, too... She looked down at the legal pad full of notes on her desk blotter, but she didn't see the page.

If only he had loved me, she thought painfully, I could have dealt with the rest. If it was just some sort of hang-up about the legal paperwork, the formal commitment of being married—— Well, lots of men feel that way. It would have disappointed me not to be a bride, but if I could have been his wife in fact, I would have done without the name, and hoped that some day he would realise...

But to be brutally told that it was only lust he felt, and that when his passion was exhausted there would be nothing left—it was that which she could not bear. It had shattered her to know that she had not really been important to him at all—that if she had not forced her way into his life some other woman would have provided his entertainment, and he would not have cared about the difference.

'Dammit!' she said as she realised she was thinking about it all over again. She gave the coffee-cup a shove. The cold liquid slopped over the legal pad, and she grabbed for a tissue to mop it up. That legal pad represented most of an afternoon spent walking through every hallway, every room of the Clinton, looking at it with eyes which had been harshly awakened just that morning when she had seen the new Kendrick Kansas City. And right now, she told herself, she'd better put her own past aside and pay a whole lot more attention to the Clinton's future—or there might not be one at all.

Bringing the hotel back to the standard it had once enjoyed was going to be a very long, very complicated, very expensive job. And Lacey wasn't at all sure she wanted to try.

* * *

After dinner that night she sought her father out in his den. 'Can I come in and talk?' she asked.

'Of course.' He laid his book aside and took his reading glasses off. 'I didn't have much of a chance to see you today,' he said. 'You were holed up in your office pretty securely. How was your tour of the Kendrick this morning?'

'Fine.' She curled up on the carpet at his feet, and put her head down on his knee.

'Beautiful, isn't it? They did a superb job of restoring the old beauty, and darned near built a whole new hotel at the same time.' He shook his head admiringly.

'Yes.' She sat up and clasped her arms around her drawn-up knees. 'Daddy, that's exactly what I want to talk to you about.'

Bill Clinton raised one eyebrow. 'You haven't called me "Daddy" in years, Lacey. As I recall, the last time you were about fifteen and in desperate trouble. What the trouble was, I don't remember, but you thought it was terrible at the time——'

She smiled. 'Well, I'm not in trouble, now. It's just that——' She paused, and decided that there was really no good way to approach this. She was just going to have to plunge in. 'Dad, you said yesterday that you sometimes regretted that you hadn't remodelled the Clinton two years ago, when Damon suggested you should.'

He looked down at his hands, folded in his lap. 'Sometimes.'

'A lot?'

'I'm not sure I know what you mean, Lacey.'

'Well, we could still do it now. If—if you'd want to.'

There was a long moment of silence. 'You think that's the best way to save the Clinton?'

'I don't know. That's the problem, Dad, there are so many things I don't know! But my instinct says if we go on the way we are, we'll just keep losing more and more guests, and soon the balance sheet is going to end in red ink instead of black——'

Bill Clinton sighed. 'I know what you're saying, Lacey.'

'But it's such an awfully big investment, and the time—it'll take a year at least, and all that time with the hotel closed, and no cash flow——' She stopped and gulped. 'And the employees—how can we just tell them we're closing for a year and to go find other jobs till we need them again? And we certainly can't keep paying them if there's no income——'

'You're not telling me anything I haven't already thought about, Lacey. I didn't toss aside the possibility lightly.'

'And doing things half-way would just be throwing money down the drain. It has to be done right, or we might as well not bother. Damon said——' She took a deep breath. 'He told me he tried to buy the Clinton.'

'We talked about it.'

'I know that the hotel is important to you, Dad——'

'Important? Lacey, I was born in that hotel. It was where my parents lived always—they never even owned a house.'

She sighed, and tried to stifle it.

'Oh, Lacey, little girl, the hotel's been my life, but I'm not foolish enough to assume that you will necessarily feel the same way.'

Hope dawned in her eyes. 'Then when you refused to sell—— '

'It was because I wanted you to have the choice. I thought perhaps when you had had time to get over Damon, you might decide to come home, and the hotel would look pretty good to you.'

She thought it over. 'What if I hadn't come back?'

'I'm not exactly decrepit, Lacey,' he pointed out drily, and she laughed. 'But I was planning to come to New York this fall to see you, and lay it all out for you. I know that something has to be done soon.'

She nodded suddenly. 'That's what it is, Dad—the feeling I get when I walk through the hotel! It's a sense of urgency, as if there isn't any time to spare. I hadn't realised——'

She broke off, and there was a long silence before Bill Clinton said gently, 'Well, my dear? Shall I call my banker tomorrow, or Damon?'

'Do you want to fight for it, Dad? It's a big job, but——'

'I asked the question first, Lacey. And you're the one who has to answer it. I may be here for five years, or ten—but it's your whole life. It's really up to you.'

She let the silence drag out for a long moment. How, she asked herself desperately, can I tell him that I don't really want the thing he has worked for all his life and tried to save and build up for me? And yet, how can I commit him to that horrible debt, and to the intense effort it will take to make it work? He's not a young man——

'Damon says it's going to get nothing but harder for an independent hotel,' she said. She was almost unaware that she had spoken.

'I'm afraid he's right.' It was matter of fact. 'And yet *harder* isn't the same as *impossible*.'

'Still——' She shook her head in despair. 'Dad, would you think I'm being a chicken if I said I'd rather have a safe job somewhere, and let someone else worry about high finance?'

Bill Clinton's smile was wry. 'Not a chicken, exactly,' he said. 'Perhaps neither of us was cut out to be an entrepreneur, Lacey.'

There were tears in her eyes. What a grand man he was, she thought. She knew how it must hurt him, to have her say this, but he was the one who was trying to comfort her!

'Then—I think you should call Damon,' she whispered.

He nodded. 'All right, my dear.' He clasped her hand.

Ginny knocked on the door just then.

'We'll have to tell your mother, of course,' he murmured. 'She's a part of this decision, too.'

Lacey nodded. Her father was the one who broke the news to Ginny; Lacey sat on the floor and stared at nothing, shredding a tissue. It sounded so much worse, she thought morosely, when her father said it. His voice was crisp, clear, as if he was talking about some other kind of business, not the one he had treasured for so many years.

When it was over, Lacey darted a fearful glance up at her mother. 'Well, I'm not surprised,' Ginny said. 'And I'm sure Damon will agree to a fair price. I'm glad to have it decided.'

That's all? Lacey thought. That's all she's going to say?

Then she saw the tears in her mother's eyes, and knew that she, too, was making a valiant effort to be brave.

'Grant's here to pick you up, Lacey,' Ginny said, and Lacey scrambled to her feet. She had almost forgotten that over coffee that morning he'd asked her to go to a new nightclub with him. At least everything was going to be all right there, she thought. At least Damon hadn't managed to mess that up for her.

'Grant's such a nice young man, I think,' Ginny said. There was still a tiny tremor in her voice, but she was smiling mistily. 'I am so glad you met him . . .'

CHAPTER FOUR

WITH the main decision made, Lacey found, it was much easier to tackle the pile of paperwork on her desk. There was no sense in agonising over a new promotional brochure, for instance, when by the time it came back from the printers the hotel would have a new owner. It might even have a new name.

She hoped her father would remember that point when he and Damon negotiated the actual sale, she thought. She might not want to run the hotel herself, but she had her share of pride in it, and she would be very sad if the day came when there was no longer a Clinton Hotel in downtown Kansas City. Surely Damon would have no reason to object to leaving the name in place, she thought, if Bill Clinton made it a condition of the sale?

But that, of course, was really her father's responsibility, and not hers. I'm just glad that I'm not the one who has to sit down with Damon and work out the details, she thought with a little shiver.

She read and signed the last few letters in the stack on her desk, and pushed them aside with a yawn. It had been a very busy week, and not only because of work, but because she had been re-establishing her old friendships and building new ones. She'd had dinner with the Pattersons one night, and she'd been seeing Grant fairly often. The day after their nightclub date he had taken her to dinner, and he'd called every day since. Tonight they were going to an open-air concert at Country Club Plaza, and if she wasn't going to be late, she realised with a glance at her wristwatch, she'd better head for home right now.

She pushed back her chair and looked admiringly at the clean, polished surface of her desk, the blotter neat, with not a stray paper in sight, and a single yellow rose in a crystal vase on the corner. It was astounding how much more easily things had gone this week...

Ginny came into her bedroom while Lacey was putting the finishing touches to her make-up. 'It's so good to have you home,' she said. 'Remember when you were tiny? You used to sit by my dressing-table and watch while I got ready to go out in the evenings. Now it's the reverse.'

Lacey laughed. 'I don't notice you staying home a lot, Ginny Clinton.'

'Mostly it's just girl-things, though. Your father's always been too busy to really get involved. Now—— You know, Lacey, when you first told me about selling the Clinton, I was really frightened. Bill's always been so absorbed in that hotel that I had no idea what he'd do with himself once he didn't have to worry about it.'

Lacey put down her eyeshadow brush. 'I know, Mother, but I'm sure that if he gives it a fair chance——'

Ginny shook her head. 'Don't sound so terrified. Now I'm really excited about the possibilities. You know we haven't had a vacation for years, Lacey, not a real one—but Bill's already talked to George and Elinor, and we're going to go to Arizona for a while next winter, to visit them and escape the worst of the cold. And he said if we like it down there we might buy a condo ourselves so we can go every winter. Just think, darling——'

There was no doubting the excitement in Ginny's voice, and the bright sparkle in her eyes was obviously no longer because of tears. Lacey released a long, relieved breath. 'I'd been afraid to think about it,' she admitted, 'for fear that he might resent me for forcing him to retire——'

'Actually, I don't think he's going to retire,' Ginny confided. 'Not completely, at any rate. I think Damon will offer him some sort of job with the chain. Bill hasn't said anything, exactly, but surely Damon won't want to let all of that experience slip away? So if Bill could work a few months a year—as a sort of consultant, or something—and then play golf all winter in the South——'

'It sounds like heaven to me.' Lacey gave her mother an impulsive hug. 'Oh, I'm so glad it's working out. I felt like a selfish beast to turn my back on the Clinton when Dad's loved it so much, and yet I just couldn't face taking on that job.'

Ginny stroked her daughter's hair. 'I know, darling. But it's going to be just fine. We're going to be so very happy, all of us.'

Ginny said it, Lacey thought, as if the weight of the world had been lifted off her shoulders, too.

Perhaps that was why it bothered her so much after the concert that night when Grant said, 'Didn't you tell me last weekend that your father is going to sell the Clinton to Hoteliers?'

Their pizza had just been set on the table between them, steaming gently and smelling deliciously of pepperoni and anchovies. Lacey burned her fingers on the cheese, stuck the tips into her mouth to soothe the pain, and said indistinctly, 'I don't think anything's been signed yet, but yes. Why?'

'Because there's been nothing said all week.'

'Well, negotiations are always kind of a sensitive thing. And even though the Clinton isn't a public company, and no one could manipulate stock or anything, I'm sure Damon has to be careful for his stockholders' sake. Don't they have rules about things like that?'

His eyes narrowed a bit. 'Yes, they do, Lacey.' He sounded a bit impatient. 'And I know all about keeping these things out of public hearing. What I mean is, there hasn't even been a hint of gossip around the corporation. Normally, when there's anything in the wind, there are rumours flying all over the country.'

Lacey took another bite of her pizza. 'Well, it is a matter between Dad and Damon,' she pointed out reasonably. 'I'd say the odds are good that they could keep a secret between them——' But would it be just the two of them? she wondered. There were surely corporate officers who would have a say, experts who would have to be consulted, lawyers to draw up papers? Damon might be the chairman of the board of Hoteliers, but he wasn't a dictator with omnipotent power...

'Kendrick's been out of town. He just got back today.'

Lacey stared at him. The slice of pizza in her hand drooped, and the cheese started to slide. She caught it just in time.

That's impossible, she thought blankly. Mother told me all about Dad's wonderful plans. He couldn't do that unless he and Damon had struck a deal, and if Damon's been gone——

They probably got it all straightened out today, she told herself. The exact price might take a while to work out, but it wouldn't take long to agree in principle on the sale. That was it, no doubt. She relaxed and began to eat her pizza.

'There have been a few rumours floating round about you, though,' Grant said. He wasn't looking at her.

'Oh?' She tried to keep her voice airy, as if it didn't matter to her what anyone thought. 'If the entire staff of the Kendrick is talking about my brief visit to Damon's penthouse, I wonder what they say about his overnight guests.'

'It's not that. Not exactly, anyway.' But he seemed unwilling to elaborate.

Lacey put her pizza down. 'Look, Grant, you can't start on a subject like this and then dance around it. Either tell me, or don't. I really don't care which it is.'

He said, as if he was issuing a challenge, 'There's some talk that you and Kendrick were engaged once, and when it broke up you ran off to New York—but that since you're home now, there must be something in the wind again.'

'Wrong. Wrong. And wrong.'

'You weren't engaged?' He looked up eagerly.

'No. And since I wasn't engaged, it follows logically that I didn't run away because of a broken engagement——' Careful, Lacey, she told herself; you're getting on to thin ice! 'In fact, I didn't run away at all, I merely took a job in New York for a while. And there is certainly no truth to the speculation that there's anything going on between us now.'

'Well——'

'If there were, wouldn't I have known Damon was out of town?'

Grant nodded. 'I suppose so.' Then he added stubbornly, 'I think you're the only person I've ever heard call him by his first name.'

'And that bothers you? I did date him, you know. It's not a crime.'

He didn't answer.

'Besides, Damon's lack of friends is more a comment on him than on me, surely. He's a very private person.'

'That's exactly why it bothers me.'

'Oh, come on, Grant. I'm sure there's a girl or two in your past. It doesn't keep me awake at night——'

'The girls in my past weren't anything like Damon Kendrick,' he said drily.

Lacey giggled. 'I should hope not.'

Grant stared at her for a split-second as if she'd gone mad, and then he started to laugh, too, and the difficult moment passed. For a little while there, Lacey thought, I was afraid he was going to get serious on me. And, though he's a perfectly nice guy, I'm certainly not ready to deal with that.

Bill and Ginny were playing pinochle in the dining-room when Lacey came in. Neither of them even looked up from their cut-throat battle, and Lacey stood in the doorway for several minutes and watched them play before saying, 'I had no idea I was home so early. Perhaps I'd better go out again for a while, so you'll miss me.'

Ginny took her eyes off her cards just long enough to say, 'If you do, dear, there's a candle in that drawer. Just set it in the front hall so it's ready for me, would you?'

Lacey laughed and pulled up a chair to watch. Eventually Bill Clinton declared himself the winner, and when the scoresheet proved him right Ginny threw in her remaining cards in disgust and went off to make some popcorn.

He pushed his chair back and rubbed his hands together in delight. 'I've been trying for the best part of my life to beat Ginny by that margin,' he said gleefully. 'And I plan to do it regularly now that I've got the time.'

It should have been all the reassurance Lacey needed, but it wasn't, somehow. 'I don't mean to nag, Dad,' she said, 'but——'

'You sound exactly like your mother, Lacey. Whenever she says that, she's just about to start.' He gathered up the cards. 'What is it, dear?'

'Have you talked to Damon yet, Dad?'

He looked her over curiously. 'And what makes you think I haven't talked to him?'

'Grant told me tonight that Damon's been out of town, that's what——'

'He's been in San Antonio,' Bill Clinton said promptly. 'I caught up with him there.'

Of course, she thought. That even explained why there hadn't been any rumours; a single telephone call—or even a series of them—wouldn't attract nearly the attention that a personal conference would. If Bill Clinton had gone over to the Hoteliers offices, the whole corporation would have heard about it by now. But a mere telephone call——

Thank heaven, she thought. She kissed the bald spot on the top of her father's head and went to bed with a much lighter heart.

I'm beginning to get paranoid, she thought, thinking that something might interfere with my perfect solution to all our problems.

And there things rested till late on Sunday afternoon. Bill and Ginny had gone to play bridge with George and Elinor Tanner. Lacey had been invited, too, but she had declined in favour of spending a couple of hours on the patio with a glass of lemonade and a good book. She settled herself in the lounge chair and began to apply sunscreen lotion with a lavish hand. Her chair was protected from the sun by the giant oak tree that overhung the house, but she knew from bitter experience how quickly a redhead could broil, even in indirect sunlight, and she'd had no opportunity to work on a tan.

She heard a car pull into the driveway and grimaced. 'Can't a girl even be undisturbed in her own back garden?' she muttered. Her blue bikini was brand new, but it was completely unsuitable for entertaining company, and she hadn't bothered to bring a cover-up outside with her. Then she decided that no rule of etiquette said she had to answer the doorbell, so she slid down into the lounge chair and opened her book instead.

Five minutes later, when a shadow fell across her, she glanced up and tried unsuccessfully to smother a groan. She put a finger on the page to mark her place. 'Dad and Mother are at a bridge party,' she said crisply. 'I'm not expecting them to be home for a couple of hours, but I'll be happy to give Dad a message, if you'd care to leave one.' She pushed her dark glasses up into her hair and raised her eyebrows enquiringly.

'I didn't come to talk to Bill,' Damon said easily. 'I wanted to see you.' He pulled a chair around, but instead of sitting down he braced his hands against the back of it and let his gaze sweep the length of her, from slender bare feet to tousled hair, and back again. 'And there is certainly a lot of you on display this afternoon——'

If I had a beach robe handy, Lacey thought, I wouldn't put it on; I'd smother him with it. She sat up and reached for the lemonade on the small table beside her. 'Well? If you have something to say, say it. If not, I'd like to keep reading.'

'I was just wondering——' He arranged the chair to give him the best possible view of her, and sat down.

'Make yourself comfortable,' Lacey said drily. 'But please remember that buying the hotel doesn't give you the right to behave as if you own this house, too.'

'The hotel,' he said, as if pleased that she'd come straight to the point. 'That's exactly what I want to talk about, Lacey. I'm confused. Where did you ever get the idea that I want to buy the Clinton?'

Her lemonade glass slid slowly from her hand and shattered against the patio. She watched the liquid pool and slowly sink into the sand between the flagstones. Then she said, as if she was talking to a toddler, 'From you, Damon. You said you'd tried to buy it two years ago.'

'Two years ago, yes—when I could have renovated it along with the Kendrick. But things change.'

'You said just a few days ago that the Kendrick wasn't big enough, that you needed more rooms.'

His eyebrows arched. 'Did I?'

'You know damned well you did!'

'Careless of me, giving away corporate plans like that.'

Her head was spinning. 'What plans are you talking about? You meant the Clinton—it was obvious!'

He shook his head. 'Well, I suppose it can't hurt to tell you, at this stage. You know that square block just west of the Kendrick?'

'The car park? Of course.'

'It would have been a damned expensive car park, if that was the only plan I had for it. We're going to break ground there in the spring and build a parking ramp and a five-hundred-room tower——'

'That's a bluff,' she said, when she got her voice back. 'I don't know what you're trying to do, other than to drive the price of the Clinton down, but if you think I am fool enough to fall for a cheap trick like that, Damon Kendrick——'

'I really don't want the Clinton at any price, Lacey.' It was calm, unemotional. 'I suppose if Bill offered to give it to me I'd take it off his hands, but I don't think that's what he's got in mind.'

'You need it!'

'No, I don't. Not now, and not at any foreseeable time. I've got a very nice, luxury-class hotel, and I'm going to put an addition on to it that will draw the kind of clients who like their hotels brand new and squeaky-clean. What could the Clinton be to me but a headache? Oh, it could be nice enough, and I suppose I could put a skywalk across the street and consider it an annex, but——'

'You told me you'd like to see it renovated,' she reminded crossly. 'You certainly can't deny saying that!'

'Yes, I would, because it would be good for the whole downtown area. I just don't particularly want to be the one who does it.'

And neither do I, Lacey thought, but perhaps he doesn't really know that. 'You're taking quite a risk, you know, Damon. If we decide to go ahead with the renovation ourselves, the Clinton will probably never be for sale again.'

'I never gamble more than I can afford to lose, Lacey. And in this case, I'm not gambling.' There was a long silence. 'I'd have bought the damned thing without a second of hesitation two years ago, but that was before we decided to go ahead with the tower. I don't need them both.'

'You said the value was there, and that——'

'Oh, I could make some money on it, but I'm not sure it would be enough to be worth the headache. And I've got a list of other projects in the works just now. I was in San Antonio to check out the site for a new airport inn, and next month I'll be in Phoenix for the grand opening of a hotel we've just finished building. There's a limit to how much expansion I can justify in a single year, Lacey.'

She almost burst into tears, as it began to register with horrifying force that he really meant what he was saying. After all, what could he possibly have to gain by turning down this opportunity if he really wanted to buy that grand old building? Certainly it was not the price that was holding him back; if it had been that, he wouldn't have said that he didn't want it no matter what the price, and in any case she was certain that her father wouldn't be adamant on the price.

Her father. He had certainly seemed to think just a couple of days ago that everything was in order, that the sale was assured.

'You told my father——' she began.

'Nothing at all,' Damon interrupted. 'He did most of the talking, and I'll admit I was in a state of shock when he tracked me down in San Antonio to accept an offer I hadn't even made.'

'Oh, heavens!' she whispered.

'I thought perhaps you and I should clear up this problem you seem to have with assuming things before I talked to Bill again.' He leaned back in his chair. The breeze ruffled his hair, and sent cold shudders through Lacey's body. 'You don't want to take on this job yourself, do you, Lacey?'

She sighed. 'I can think of a lot of things I'd sooner do, yes.' Then she caught herself up short. 'But that doesn't mean I won't do it! You'll see——'

'Oh, at least be honest. You don't want to dirty your hands with it, and I can't say that I blame you. I also got the feeling from your father that even he felt a bit of relief at the prospect of handing it over to me.'

She wasn't about to confirm that. But neither could she honestly deny it, so she sat still with her lips compressed, and just looked at him.

'But my intuition says it's really you who wants me to do it,' he mused. 'As if there's something you know about that I don't—like a structural crack in the lobby ceiling that will bring the whole hotel down on my hapless head the first time I walk in——'

'There's nothing,' she said sullenly. 'You surely can't believe my father would try to sell you a building that was faulty?'

'No, but you might.' He looked at her through lazy-lidded eyes and said, 'I find it fascinating that everyone seems to think I'll be unable to refuse this challenge. In fact, Lacey, I can only think of one thing that would tempt me to do it.'

The silence dragged out until it was painful. Lacey licked her lips. She hated herself for asking, because it was so obvious that he wanted her to. 'What's that?'

He looked up at the shifting patterns of tree branches above his head. 'The gratitude you would feel if I bailed you out.' His voice was low and indolent.

'I don't quite understand...'

He turned his head and smiled at her. 'Come on, Lacey. You never used to be lacking in imagination. When I think of the ways you could find to express your appreciation——'

She gasped and sat bolt upright in the lounge chair. 'Damon Kendrick, you're a filthy-minded beast!'

'Careful, Lacey,' he warned. 'I'm not sure that bikini will stand the strain if you get any more upset.'

'You've got a nerve! Carrying on like this, telling me you didn't want the hotel, just so you could try to bluff me into your bed——'

His voice cut coolly across the tirade. 'I'm not bluffing, Lacey. If I take on the Clinton, it will be as a personal favour to you. And I am not accustomed to doing favours without getting favours in return.'

She started to laugh. 'You know, this is really a pathetic joke.'

'No joke about it.'

'The very idea that I would prostitute myself——' She sputtered to a halt.

'Don't you think that's putting it a little strongly? It's not as if you wouldn't have a good time. You know quite well, Lacey, that you would enjoy going to bed with me. Two years ago your prudish moral code kept you from doing it. Now——'

She swallowed hard, feeling as if she was fighting for her sanity. 'You're a better businessman than that,' she said desperately. 'You didn't get where you are by basing business decisions on something as crass as your own lust.'

'No,' he said coolly. 'I didn't. Don't kid yourself that I'm willing to make a company sacrifice to have you. I'm not about to put my head on the block with my board of directors; if I buy the Clinton, you can bet that it'll end up being a profit-maker.'

She seized on the fragment of hope. 'Then why drag me into it at all? Either you want it or you don't!'

'Because it really doesn't matter to me whether I get the Clinton or not. It's a marginal decision, and I'm inclined to turn it down simply because there are too many other opportunities right now to make that one worth my time. But you're the thing that could tip the balance, Lacey.'

She felt as if her chest was so compressed that she would never be able to draw another breath.

'Because, you see, I do still want you.'

It was cool and precise, she thought in horror, as if he was talking about a new car or a piece of furniture!

The silence stretched out interminably.

'I suppose I should be flattered,' she said stiffly, thinking of the woman he'd brought to her party. 'Your standards in women are going up.'

'I don't know about that. You've been in my head for a long time.' He looked completely relaxed, sitting in the comfortable lounge chair, as if the proposition he had just made was a matter of complete indifference to him. He wasn't even looking at her; he seemed to be admiring a cardinal in the top of the oak tree.

She said, sarcastically, 'And I suppose you'd like to take care of implementing this little arrangement right now. My parents won't be back for a couple of hours. It's a perfect opportunity.'

He turned his head lazily and looked at her, and then got out of his chair. 'If you like,' he said equably. In little more than a step he was beside her, bending to pick her up out of her chair.

She struggled in his arms. 'No!' It was only a hoarse whisper; she had no strength left to scream. 'I didn't agree to it, I didn't——'

'It certainly sounded to me as if you did.' He kicked the back door open and carried her into the wide hallway. He let her slide slowly till her toes barely touched the floor, and every square inch of her skin protested as the heat of his body scorched her. The tiny wisps of her bikini were no protection at all against the pressure of his hands forcing her against him, moulding her muscles to the hard contours of his. His mouth came down on hers without gentleness, in a harsh and demanding kiss that cut off what might have been a shriek, or only a frightened whimper.

Then he let her go, so suddenly that she staggered and would have crumpled to the floor if his hands hadn't closed again on her upper arms and held her steady.

'I'm sorry if I've disappointed you,' he said. He was breathing raggedly. 'But actually, I didn't bring you in here to ravish you today. I just carried you in so you wouldn't cut your beautiful toes on the broken glass out there.'

It took a moment for the relief to soak through her. 'I knew you couldn't mean that horrible suggestion,' she whispered. 'Damon——'

'Oh, I mean it. And as for this afternoon, and your invitation...'

'It wasn't an invitation!'

'I could make love to you right now with the greatest of pleasure. But I told you once that it's going to take considerably more than a one-night stand before I get tired of you, and I'm not going to risk losing that. When you come to me, Lacey——'

'I won't,' she said hotly. 'I still have options, you know!'

'You will come to me.' His voice was like the soothing whisper of a hypnotist. 'Because you want to know what we could be like together.'

He pulled her against him, more gently this time. His lips were soft and tender, and yet this kiss was every bit as threatening. Her muscles wouldn't work properly, she realised foggily. Nothing about her was functioning correctly. Her arms seemed to want to go around his neck...

He raised his head. 'That's just to remind you,' he said huskily, 'that being my mistress wouldn't be such a terrible thing for you, after all.'

Then he was gone.

Lacey sagged against the wall. Even with that support, her legs wouldn't hold her up, and she slid down to the hard oak floor in a crumpled heap. She sat there for a long time, knowing that she must get up, that she had to pull herself together before her parents came home.

Dear heaven, she thought, what am I going to tell my parents?

CHAPTER FIVE

LACEY was absolutely astounded that Bill and Ginny didn't seem to notice anything wrong with her. They came home overflowing with plans for all the things they were going to do when winter came, and settled themselves at the dining-room table with a stack of *Arizona Highways* magazines, a guidebook, and a map—all borrowed from George and Elinor Tanner.

Lacey retreated to the far end of the house and turned the television set on. Even there, she couldn't entirely escape; Bill Clinton kept drifting in to read her bits from the guidebook, until finally she could stand no more.

She knew that she could not say anything to them tonight; she had to have a chance to think first. It wasn't that she had any intention of taking Damon up on his insulting and horrifying proposition, but there had to be a way, she thought, of telling Bill and Ginny with reasonable gentleness that the hotel would not be sold, after all. It was just going to take some calm thought to find it, that was all, and so she turned off the comedy that she'd been mindlessly staring at and went to say goodnight to her parents.

Ginny looked at her with startled concern. 'But it's so early, darling. Did you get too much sun today?' she asked solicitously. 'Perhaps an aspirin and a cool bath would help.'

There aren't enough pain-killers and gallons of water in the world to help, Lacey thought, unless I take an overdose or drown myself...

'Would you like me to come up and rub your back?'

She shook her head emphatically and made a quick escape, and didn't know whether to be glad or sorry that her mother didn't follow her upstairs. She was happy not to have to deal with any more questions, of course, but, on the other hand, if the thought of Arizona was casting such a strong lure that it could actually overcome Ginny's maternal instinct, it was going to be even harder to tell her that it now lay out of her reach.

But the quiet darkness of Lacey's own room was no more conducive to thought than the senseless noise of the television had been. Every time she closed her eyes she could feel the urgent pressure of Damon's mouth against hers, and the way his body had seemed to burn an impression on to her soft skin. And, though she finally slept, it was to wake with a jerk, over and over again, from dreams that she couldn't quite remember, but which she knew she would not want to analyse even if she could recall the details.

In the morning she looked five years older. 'As if I'm due for a facelift,' she told her mirror. 'Well, that's one sure way to handle Damon—keep this up for a couple of weeks, and he won't be interested any more.'

The problem was, she might not have a couple of weeks. He hadn't put a deadline on his offer, but the matter couldn't be left hanging in limbo for long, or Bill Clinton was going to start asking questions. And before that time came Lacey knew she not only had to figure out what she was going to tell him about the sale falling through, but some alternative plan for the hotel as well.

So she left a note on the breakfast-table for her mother, who was still asleep, and went to work at an hour when the sun was still peering weakly over the horizon.

The yellow rose in the crystal vase on her desk had drooped and died over the weekend. 'Poor thing,' Lacey said. 'You didn't have a fair chance, either, did you?' She touched it with a gentle finger, and a couple of withered petals dropped on to the blotter. This, she thought, is what Damon would do to me. Not that he would intend to, exactly—but the effect would be the same.

She took from her desk drawer the folder that held the notes she had made last week about the renovation project, and started all over again.

When her father's secretary tapped on the door a couple of hours later, Lacey was so absorbed in her calculations that she didn't hear. The secretary put her head in. 'Miss Clinton, there's a telephone call for you. And I've got those statistics you wanted.'

Lacey put her pen down reluctantly and reached automatically for the telephone. 'Who's calling?' she asked belatedly.

'Mr Kendrick.'

Lacey wanted to swear. But she had already lifted the receiver; it was too late to instruct the woman to tell him that Miss Clinton had just stepped out to Tahiti, and she'd be back in a year or two...

The secretary picked up the crystal vase. 'I'll get rid of this for you.'

'No! Leave it.' The secretary looked stunned at the sharp tone of Lacey's voice, so she said, more gently, 'I think I'll press it. It's sort of a special rose——'

'What colour is it?' Damon asked. His voice seemed to tickle her ear.

'Why on earth would you want to know?'

'Because in case it was a man who gave it to you, I wouldn't want to repeat his gesture.'

'Believe me, Damon,' she said crossly, 'I'm not likely to confuse you with anyone else.'

He laughed. 'Good. Let's keep it that way. Have you made up your mind yet?'

She tightened her grip on the telephone, and wished that it was his throat. 'Yes,' she said politely. 'Remember? I told you yesterday that I'm not interested.'

'Oh, you're interested all right. But we won't argue that. Obviously you haven't talked to your father this morning.'

Her voice came out in a sort of horrified squeak. 'Do you mean you have?'

'Oh, it wasn't much more than a social call. Don't worry; I didn't tell him anything about our discussion yesterday.'

'Then what did you tell him?'

'Why don't you ask Bill? Of course, you should be careful not to arouse his curiosity too much, unless you plan to bare your soul altogether.'

'It would serve you right if I did tell him about your indecent little offer!'

'But you aren't going to, or you would have already done it. Why haven't you told him, anyway? An interesting question—I've been thinking about it all morning. I'm going to be out of the office today, Lacey, but I'll instruct my secretary that if you call, it's of the ultimate importance that she find me, no matter what.'

'Don't bother. I'm not going to call, today or ever.'

'I'll tell her anyway. Just in case,' he said softly, and then there was only the soft buzz of a dead line against her ear.

She slammed the telephone receiver down so hard she thought she'd broken it, and stormed down the hall to her father's office. At the door she paused and gave herself a mental shake. 'You can't go flying in there like a team of inquisitors,' she muttered, and took a deep breath. Tact, that was what was going to be required here.

Bill Clinton was reading the latest issue of a hotel-management publication. At least, Lacey thought, it wasn't *Arizona Highways*!

She dropped into the chair beside his desk and said, 'You know, Dad, I've been thinking a lot the past few days. And I've decided that perhaps I was being a little hasty last week in deciding to get out of the hotel business.'

Bill Clinton's eyebrows climbed steeply up his forehead. 'Don't you think it's a bit late for second thoughts?' he asked reasonably. 'Damon's not going to be happy if you change your mind.'

Daddy, she thought, you don't know the half of it!

She took a deep breath. 'When I think about it, I realise that I didn't give the renovation fair consideration. Surely it wouldn't hurt to look into it a little further? We should talk to the bankers, at least. Even if we decided in the end not to go ahead with it ourselves, having the information couldn't hurt. It would certainly make the deal look better to a buyer——'

'But we have a buyer, Lacey. And knowing Damon and his habit of being ready for all possibilities, he probably had all the blueprints drawn two years ago. Why go to all that effort to duplicate his work?'

Lacey swallowed hard. 'Well, why should we limit ourselves to one possible buyer?' she asked determinedly. 'There are other chains. One of Damon's competitors might bid more, just to take it away from him. Not for the sake of thumbing their noses at him, exactly, but because it's the best way to compete with him right on his own territory.'

'Lacey, I don't know why you've suddenly decided Damon shouldn't have this hotel, but——'

'I'm not sure I trust him, that's all. Has he told you what he plans to do with it?'

'Not exactly. But I wouldn't expect him to, until the papers are signed.'

'See? He might just skip the renovation and turn it into——' She rummaged around in her mind, but she couldn't think of anything quite horrible enough.

'A house of ill fame?' Bill Clinton asked with a wry smile. 'No, Lacey. He told me just this morning that he was sure I'd be happy with the outcome.'

Lacey closed her eyes in pain.

'Daddy, please,' she whispered. 'Let's talk to the bankers, at least. It's not as if you've already made a deal with Damon, after all.'

He looked at her for a long moment. 'You know how much I've always hated to refuse you, don't you, Lacey? Very well—if it will make you feel better, we'll talk to the bankers. But I think it would only be fair to warn Damon that we're having second thoughts about selling.'

That ought to amuse him greatly, Lacey thought bitterly.

The group of vice-presidents of First Federal Bank who were gathered in the conference room in the gleaming new glass and steel building represented more lending power than Lacey had ever dreamed it was possible to put together at one table. She knew that winning them over would be a public relations victory larger and more important than any she had ever attempted before, and she had spent two days gathering her figures and rehearsing her presentation until it was letter-perfect. Now, as she drew to a conclusion, she pushed her papers together, folded her hands on top of them and looked around the room, meeting the eyes of each of the five men and two women in turn.

'Ladies and gentlemen,' she said, and let her voice drop to a soft, compelling plea, 'I speak of the need for this renovation project out of personal knowledge. I spent last night as a guest in the Clinton Hotel, experiencing the same things that our guests do. And I must tell you honestly that by the standards of today's traveller, the Clinton no longer has the edge of comfort and elegance that it always has boasted. Last night I dis covered——'

Last night, she thought, while her words went on smoothly in that well-rehearsed speech. The very mention of last night was like a thorn in her side. For one thing, as soon as she had time, she intended to find out which of the Clinton's employees was doubling as Damon Kendrick's spy. It was obvious that he had one; how else could he have learned that she was spending the night in the hotel?

She had been curled up with her notes, sipping a cup of almost-hot room-service tea, when the bedside telephone rang shortly before midnight. She answered a bit warily, thinking it might be the front desk with a problem.

Damon said, 'So you took my suggestion to check the hotel out first-hand, did you?'

'And how did you happen to hear about it?'

'You know how information flies in this business. I hope you're having a pleasant stay.'

'To be honest, not particularly. The bathroom is damned inconvenient, and there's no reading light by the bed. When I rip into this place, you can bet that I'll make sure——'

'I could come over,' he said promptly. 'I can't do much about the bathroom, but if I were there you wouldn't need the reading light.'

'Thanks, anyway,' Lacey said tartly.

'Besides, two heads are better than one when it comes to looking for problems, and since most people travel in pairs, you could really get the full effect that way.

For example, it's hard to tell if a bed is comfortable for two people, if there's only one in it——'

She had hung up on him, but she'd had the uncomfortable feeling that he'd been laughing at her all the time...

Stop it, Lacey warned herself. You can't afford to be thinking about Damon Kendrick just now.

There was no doubt that she had the full attention of every banker in the room. She paused for a breath, and then said, 'What my father and I are offering you is a chance to be a part of the rebirth of an important, historical part of Kansas City. I'll be honest; the easy way would be for us to sell the Clinton to a chain which would depreciate it, let it run down, and then abandon it. Instead, with your help, we are willing to make the personal and financial investment necessary to bring it back to the grandeur it possessed on opening day. It can be—it will be—grand again.'

There was a brief silence. It didn't bother Lacey, exactly; she knew that it would take a while for them to consider everything she had said. And yet, she hoped that someone would say something soon. She sipped from the glass of water at her elbow and watched. The young man at the corner of the table had almost been applauding, she thought. Now, if only the rest of them felt that way, she could call up Damon Kendrick as soon as she got back to the Clinton and tell him to jump off the top of that brand new tower he said he was going to build...

'All of that is very affecting,' the senior vice-president said. His voice was a dry rasp. 'You're a dynamic speaker, Miss Clinton, but I'm afraid some of these numbers you've given us aren't quite as convincing.' He tapped an index finger on the papers in front of him. 'The amount you've budgeted for renovation costs, for example.'

'It isn't a precise figure, of course. We're only asking for preliminary approval today,' Lacey pointed out. 'But that is an architect's estimate of what it would cost to completely rehabilitate the building.' And the trouble I had, she thought, in getting those numbers in such a short time...

He shook his head in dissatisfaction. 'Even assuming that it's accurate, it seems to me that you're overlooking some things.'

There was a murmur around the table, and Lacey felt a cold trickle of doubt travel the length of her spine.

The questions came in a barrage. Were they really being realistic in projecting the huge increase in occupancy rates that it would take to repay the loan? What about the rumours that the Hoteliers Corporation was going to put up an addition to the Kendrick Kansas City—wouldn't that create a glut of downtown hotel rooms, and make them all less valuable?

Bill Clinton looked at her sharply, but he kept silent.

Wouldn't it be important to somehow increase the amount of parking space for guests? What would happen if the work couldn't be entirely completed in the year she was planning on?

Now, she thought, I know what it feels like to face a firing squad.

With two years yet to run on the employees' contract, was their union going to be a problem? And what about her own inexperience in hotel management? Wasn't she taking on a project that even an experienced manager might well turn down?

No, it's not a firing squad, she thought in desperation. It's a school of piranhas, nibbling at my flesh...

It seemed hours before the senior vice-president said, 'We'll take this under consideration, of course, and study the figures you've given us in more depth. But you wanted an indication of our answer today.' He sighed.

'I'm afraid as things stand now I would have to recommend against the issuing of this loan. The risk is just too large. Of course, if you could give us some sort of additional security, or if another bank would agree to share the loan, so First Federal would not have to assume all the risk——'

Lacey managed to smile and thank him for his time, and she didn't explode until they were safely out of the bank. Then she slammed both fists against the steering-wheel of her car and stormed, 'Now I know why they call Missouri the Show-Me State! I can't believe they asked for additional security when we're already putting up the Clinton itself as collateral! "The risk is just too large"—what about the risk we're taking?'

'I'd say they think that's the problem,' Bill Clinton said drily. 'Well, it wasn't a final rejection, but——'

'Of course it wasn't. They didn't turn us down flat because they knew we'd get the message. If we go back with more security, they'll find another reason. They aren't about to give us that money, Dad, and you know it.'

He sighed. 'Are you satisfied, now that you've tried, Lacey? Now are you going to be reasonable about selling the Clinton to Damon?'

She fought off the cold terror that was seeping into her heart, and scoffed, 'Because a few pin-striped fuddy-duddies don't have the sense to recognise a good thing when they see it?'

It had a vaguely familiar ring. What was it Damon had said? Something about it being a challenge to find a banker with vision enough to see the possibilities. But he'd had no doubt that it could be done, or at least that he could do it.

'I'm not giving up, Dad,' she said stubbornly. 'Maybe there's a venture capital company that would be interested.'

Bill Clinton grunted. 'What's this about a tower Damon's going to build?'

'How should I know?' Lacey said crossly. She heard the faint sound of a siren, and rolled her window down. It was so hard, in the cavernous streets of a city, to tell what direction an emergency vehicle was going. Besides, it made a good excuse for not listening to her father, and she had a feeling she wasn't going to like what he had to say.

'Lacey.' Bill Clinton's voice was no longer the indulgent tone of a parent, but the hard-edged sternness of an employer. 'Have you been telling me less than the truth? Is Damon backing out?'

She stole a glance at him. He looked a little pale, she thought, and worn out. And who could blame him?

A fire engine screeched down the cross street in front of them. Lacey hit the brakes just in time to avoid entering the path of a second fire engine as it, too, careened through the intersection against the traffic light. From the distance, she could hear the wavering scream of more sirens approaching. She turned the corner cautiously and halted as a policeman waved her over. 'You can't get through,' he said.

'I'm just going to the Clinton Hotel. It's right there——' Then reality struck deep into her heart. The trucks had stopped, and firemen were swarming around them and under the dark green canopy over the hotel's front door. It was the Clinton that was on fire.

She shot a look at her father's face, stricken and grey. 'I've got to get there,' she said desperately. 'I'm Lacey Clinton, and my father owns the hotel——'

'Lady, I don't care if you're the Pope's mother, you can't take this car any further. Turn it around.'

'It's a one-way street,' she protested, without even realising what she was saying.

Bill Clinton flung the car door open and darted off down the street at a run. Lacey shot a glance around, then backed the car over the kerb with a bounce and into the Kendrick's car park—the future site of a brand-new hotel tower, she thought. After today, Damon might be able to buy a quarter-block across the street pretty cheaply, too. He might even turn it into a car park to replace the one he was building on.

Her eyes began to sting, and she furiously blinked the tears away. There was going to be no time for that sort of weakness today.

One of the Kendrick's car park attendants called, 'Hey, you can't just—— Oh, it's you, Miss Clinton.'

She flung her car keys at him without a word and ran towards the Clinton. The sirens had died in mid-scream, or else they were simply being drowned out by the hotel's own fire alarm, shrieking a steady, eardrum-piercing note.

Her heart was pounding and she was labouring for breath as she pushed through the crowd of curious by-standers, and there was a horribly brassy taste in her mouth as she reached the shelter of the front canopy.

A harsh, acrid smell hung in the air, but there was no visible smoke. A fire hose snaked across the pavement and into the lobby, spitting water where it was attached to the hydrant. At the front door, two policemen were holding back a television cameraman who obviously wanted to go inside.

Lacey went up to them. 'I'm the public relations director. Have all the guests been evacuated?'

One of the policemen nodded and gestured across the street to a group of hotel guests, huddled on the pavement. 'Public relations, hmm? Looks like you've got a job ahead of you.'

Lacey shuddered. 'How bad is it?'

'The fire's out. It was just a small blaze in the coffee-shop kitchen. I guess the sprinkler got most of it before the trucks even got here. Only minor damage.'

She took one quick look into the lobby, and gulped. This is what they call minor? she thought. 'May I go in?'

'Do you have identification?' She fumbled for her hotel badge, and he nodded. She stepped carefully over the fire hose and walked through the deserted main lobby.

She found her father in the small coffee-shop off the corner of the lobby, talking to a fire official. Water was still dripping from the sprinkler heads in the ceiling on to tables that had been neatly set, waiting for the lunch crowd. She looked down at what had once been a picture-perfect cheeseburger and french fries on a table near the kitchen door and shuddered.

'It could have been a lot worse, you know.' The voice beside her was even, unemotional.

Lacey nearly jumped out of her skin. She wheeled around and stared up with shock-wide eyes. 'Well, I might have known you'd turn up!' she said venomously. 'Did you come to press your advantage, Damon?'

'It hadn't occurred to me.' His dark brown eyes were cool.

'Well, I'd like to know how you got in,' she said pettishly. 'Or didn't they ask the great Mr Kendrick for identification at the door?'

He looked down at her for a long moment. 'Actually, I came to see what sort of help you're going to need. Unless you have half a dozen people on standby to deal with a situation like this, you can't afford to be rude to volunteers, Lacey.'

Bill Clinton turned away from the fire official and came quickly across the room with his hand outstretched. His voice was choked with tears as he said, 'Damon, you're a man in a million.'

Lacey bit her lip, and then said huskily, 'You're right, Damon; we're going to need all the help we can get.'

'A little ungracious for an apology,' he mused, 'but better than nothing. I think, to start with, we could use an extra desk clerk and a couple of bellboys, don't you?' He went off to call the Kendrick Kansas City for reinforcements.

For the rest of the afternoon she worked almost side by side with him at a table set up at the dry end of the lobby. She felt like a broken record as over and over again she explained the circumstances, pacified the concerns of guests, arranged other accommodation for those whose rooms had been smoke-damaged or who were simply panicky about staying in the Clinton. There were astonishingly few of the latter, Lacey thought, until she realised the effect that Damon's soothing words were having. After that, she passed along the troublesome ones to him. Her own nerves were screaming, and if he was so good at it, she thought wearily, let him do it.

Some time about mid-afternoon—it felt to Lacey as if it should be well into the night by then—her father finished with the first round of fire inspectors and stopped beside the table where they were working. 'It was electrical, of course,' he said. 'I suppose the whole hotel is emptying out.'

'No, I think we've got it under control,' Damon said. 'Bill, you look exhausted. Why don't you go home?'

Lacey took a good look at her father. He looked a good deal worse than exhausted, she thought privately. There were streaks of dirt and smoke and water all over what had been a very elegant silver-grey suit. Worse, he was pale, and beads of sweat stood out on his forehead, and his hands were trembling like those of a very old man. When he realised that she had spotted the shaking, he jammed his fingers in his pockets and tried to smile.

He had looked worn even before the fire, she remembered guiltily, after that session with the bankers.

'No,' he said. 'I'd better——'

'Lacey and I can manage the rest, and you'll be needed even more tomorrow, or whenever the clean-up can start. We'll find someone to drive you home.' Damon glanced around the lobby and then went in search of a bellboy.

Bill Clinton grinned shakily. 'That young man doesn't take no for an answer, does he?'

'He's making sure of his investment, I suppose.'

He pulled a chair around and sat down beside her. 'Lacey,' he said very quietly, 'that's unworthy of you.'

She bit her tongue, a little ashamed of herself. Having the extra help had made all the difference today, she knew that. If it hadn't been for Damon, they wouldn't have a single guest left.

Bill Clinton looked around at the almost deserted lobby, its lovely carpets still dark with water stains, and murmured, 'I didn't realise how tired I was.'

She looked at the worn face. There were lines deeply engraved into his cheeks and brow. She thought, with a sort of frozen horror, he looks tired enough to just lie down and die.

'Lacey, you will be sensible, won't you? No more nonsense about bankers——'

Sensible, she thought. But if the cost for her father's peace of mind was her own sacrifice...?

Common sense told her that she couldn't tell him now about the price Damon had demanded; coming on top of everything else, it might well be the final blow. So it was up to her.

Once, she had actually been eager to share Damon Kendrick's bed. For her father's sake, could she bear to pay the price?

'All right, Dad,' she whispered. 'I won't fight it any more.'

Damon's shadow fell across the table. 'Lacey's car is out front,' he said. 'The parking attendant brought it back after things quieted down. But I can't seem to find anyone who's free to drive you.'

'I'm all right now,' Bill said. He patted Lacey's hand and stood up. 'I'll come back after you later, dear. Just call when you're finished here.'

'I'll see that she gets home,' Damon said quietly.

She felt as if the jaws of a trap had quietly closed around her. He hasn't said when he's planning to take me home, she thought, half hysterically. In a week or two? A month? Whenever the enchantment wears off?

She watched her father cross the lobby and disappear. 'You win, Damon. The Clinton——' She swallowed hard. 'And everything else, too.'

Damon glanced around and shrugged his shoulders, as if it didn't look much like a victory to him just now.

Fear began to trickle down her spine. What if, after all, he threw the deal in her face now? How could she go back to her father and tell him——

Her hand closed on his sleeve in desperation. 'I know it looks horrible,' she said. 'But it really is minor, and if you're going to tear the place apart anyway, it won't matter.' You're chattering, she told herself. Stop it!

He looked down at her, and there was a glint of humour in his dark eyes. 'You sound as if you're trying to convince me,' he said softly. 'Lacey, darling——'

'Believe me, Damon——' she began hotly.

He cut firmly across her words. 'You'll join me for dinner tonight, won't you, my dear? I believe we've got some things to talk over.'

CHAPTER SIX

WHAT had seemed an endless afternoon drew to a close with frightening swiftness after that. The last inspectors left. The security people locked doors and set up barricades to protect the careless and the curious who might wander into the fire scene. The last guest was eventually soothed and resettled, and then there was no excuse left for Lacey to remain in the Clinton's lobby any longer.

But when she rose from the table it was with reluctance. 'I don't know,' she said. 'Perhaps I should stay here tonight. There could be problems, and the night manager——'

'The night manager has been on the job for eighteen years, Lacey.' Damon's tone was dry. 'And I've briefed him about what to do if there is trouble. I think you can feel secure about leaving.'

She frowned unhappily. 'You'll take me home to change clothes, won't you? I'm all smoky, and if we're going out——'

'We're only going to my apartment. Humphrey won't be offended.'

To his apartment. Well, what had she expected? 'Can I at least change clothes? I've still got my overnight bag here from last night.'

'Bring it along. I've got a shower.'

She was almost in tears. 'Dammit, Damon, I don't want to walk through the lobby of the Kendrick with you, carrying a suitcase!'

He shrugged. 'Who'd pay attention? It is a hotel.'

'*Everybody* would see! Will you at least let me keep my pride?'

'Is it your pride that's bothering you, or the fear that I might want to share your shower?' There was a teasing tone to his voice.

She sniffed and refused to look at him.

He pushed a loose lock of hair behind her ear with a proprietorial hand. It seemed to Lacey that the careless gesture marked her as his property even more blatantly than an embrace would have. 'Run along,' he said. 'I'll wait here.'

With all the confusion of the day, the room she had used the night before still hadn't been made up. She scrubbed herself till she thought she'd removed a full layer of skin before she was sure she'd banished all the smoke, and then stood toweling her hair dry with one hand while she dialled the telephone with the other one.

Ginny answered on the second ring. 'Shall I come and get you after all, dear?'

I wish you could, Lacey thought. 'I may be late, Mother. I'm having dinner with Damon.'

'Oh, it's nice of him to take your mind off the fire. Perhaps we can have a cup of tea together when you get home and you can tell me about it. Your father hasn't had much to say.'

'Umm—Mother, I meant that I may be very late.' She bit her lip. No etiquette book that she had ever seen had touched on the rules for handling this sort of subject with one's mother. By the time this is over, she thought, I could probably write one.

'Well, I'm sure you and Damon will have a lot to talk about. I'll leave the porch light on for you if I go to bed before you're home.'

Lacey gave up.

'Your father's had a nap and he's looking much better now. I can't say enough for your good sense in sending him home this afternoon, Lacey.'

'Yes,' Lacey said drearily. 'Well, that's a relief. I'm glad to hear that he was just over-tired, and not sick.'

'It was the shock, I think,' Ginny agreed. 'Tell Damon I said you need your rest tonight, too.'

That, Lacey thought, would be the last message I'd pass on. He'd probably have Humphrey serve dinner in bed...

She put on the jeans and cotton sweater that she had brought to lounge around her hotel room last night. The outfit was not exactly glamorous, but it was better than the smoke-scented linen suit she'd taken off. Besides, she thought, even if she'd had her whole wardrobe to choose from, she'd have had a hard time dressing appropriately. Nothing she owned was suitable to wear to an orgy...

Damon's apartment was cool and quiet and dimly lit, with soft curtains drawn over the long windows to filter out the blistering heat of the still-high sun.

'Humphrey, get Miss Clinton a drink, please, while I go and have a shower.' Damon vanished down the hall, and Lacey accepted a glass of white wine and settled into a low chair with a sigh. At least he hadn't invited her to join him.

Time was playing tricks on her again. At the moment, she felt as if a day or two had passed since she had heard the first siren, but it was barely seven o'clock. Now, at least, she would have a few minutes of peace and quiet, before she had to deal with Damon again...

She didn't hear him come back into the room. He stood for a long moment and looked down at her, relaxed in the chair with her lashes heavy against her cheeks. When he gently took the full wineglass out of her hand, she murmured something and then curled her fingers around a cushion and turned her face into it. And when she stirred a long time later and sat up, it was to see him stretched out in a chair opposite her, silently drinking wine and watching her. He had changed his dark blue suit for casual trousers and an open-necked shirt with the sleeves rolled up. His hair had curled into little ringlets as it dried, and she tried uneasily to judge how long she must have been asleep.

'About an hour,' Damon said easily, as if he'd read her mind. 'You looked as if you needed it. I was about to wake you up, though. Humphrey's been having fits and telling me that dinner will be spoiled if we don't eat soon.'

'It's nice of him to do it so quietly,' Lacey said uncertainly. 'Have fits, I mean. Damon, we really need to talk——'

'After dinner.' He offered a hand to pull her out of the deep, soft chair. She pretended not to see it. She was furious with herself for going to sleep, and losing this opportunity to talk to him. She was afraid that after dinner, it might not be so easy...

And there certainly was no chance during the meal, with Humphrey hovering. It was a wonderful dinner, Lacey thought, enough to tempt even her sadly lacking appetite. There was a light, clear soup to start, followed by broiled swordfish with a wonderful lime sauce and a green salad with a light, tangy dressing.

'It's Humphrey's own recipe,' Damon told her lightly. 'He's so wonderful, if he ever takes another job I'll run myself through with his best carving knife.' Then he refilled her champagne glass and turned the conversation back to theatre. Surely, he said, she'd had a chance to see some plays on Broadway...

Clean living, Lacey thought. No wonder there isn't an extra ounce of weight on him. He's a man of simple tastes. He likes his food well-prepared but not fussy, and his women close at hand, without the complications of permanent relationships.

It gave her a sudden queasy feeling, and she shook her head at the moulded chocolate basket of raspberries and light cream which Humphrey offered for dessert. Almost instantly she wished that she had accepted it instead; surely she could have toyed with it and drawn the meal out for another half-hour or so, but the chance was gone. And now the reckoning was due...

'We'll have our coffee in the library, Humphrey.' Damon pushed his chair back. There was nothing for Lacey to do but follow his lead.

The room he led her to was a surprise. It was lined with bookcases, each protected by tightly fitted glass doors. Some were locked. This was no random grouping of reading material, but a studied collection of authors and of rare editions. For a moment, she let herself forget the circumstances and browsed the shelves with delight. 'Damon, I had no idea that you collected books!' she exclaimed. 'You certainly didn't have a library before.'

'I didn't have an extra room,' he said briefly. 'And since you never allowed yourself to get as far as my bedroom, you never saw these.'

She coloured a little and turned back to the shelves. You should have expected that, Lacey, she told herself. Every time you open your mouth you get into trouble.

Humphrey brought the coffee-tray in and arranged it on a low, octagonal table in the centre of the room.

'Miss Clinton will pour,' Damon said. 'That will be all for tonight, Humphrey. Thank you.'

Reluctantly, she took her place behind the china coffee-service. She didn't have to ask whether he still took his coffee black; he'd been drinking it that way all afternoon, from the big pots the Kendrick's restaurant had sent down...

He leaned back in the leather chair, the cup and saucer balanced on his knee, and looked across at her. 'Of course, this time it will be different,' he said dreamily.

It made her feel like a housefly hopelessly caught in a web, with a spider nearby—a spider who wasn't hungry just yet, but who was contemplating his next meal, and beginning to salivate...

Her hand shook a little as she poured her own coffee. A little caffeine, she thought, might help chase away the odd feeling of unreality that the champagne had left. 'Damon,' she said. 'There are some things I have to talk to you about.'

'Oh?'

It was only a murmur, and not an encouraging one, but she knew there would not be another chance. 'There are some terms I need to make clear,' she said. 'Things that I absolutely must be assured of.'

'And I thought you were the one who surrendered.'

She tried to ignore him. 'The hotel,' she said. 'It's always been a first-class operation, and I want your word of honour that it always will be.'

He didn't answer.

'No cheap remodelling, no re-selling it to a budget chain.'

There was still no response. He sipped his coffee and looked at her enquiringly.

'And its name has to stay. I mean that it's always to have "Clinton" in its title—— What did you say?'

He put his cup down. 'I was merely thinking that these sound more like non-negotiable demands than requests thrown on the table for discussion. I suppose you also want to be the general manager for life, with no provisions for removing you.'

'No. I've had my fill of making management decisions. And in any case, once our——' She stopped, her voice choked. 'Once this arrangement is over, I don't think I'd want to be working for you.'

'Why do you have so much trouble saying the words "love affair", Lacey?'

'I suppose because there's no love about it, that's why! And there's one more thing, Damon, or the deal's off.'

'Oh? And what is that?'

She set her cup down and clasped her hands on her knees. Her fingers were trembling. She didn't look at him. 'I can't face my parents and tell them what I'm doing, and why. I want your solemn promise that they will never know the price I paid.'

There was a long silent moment. 'That would be a bit inconvenient, don't you think?' He sounded matter-of-fact.

'What do you mean, inconvenient?'

'Well, I can't quite see myself rappelling up the outside of your house every night and climbing through your bedroom window.'

She snapped, 'Surely you don't expect me to tell my mother, "Goodnight, and don't expect me till breakfast, because I'm going over to sleep with Damon"?'

'Not exactly,' he mused.

'I should hope not! You've always seemed to have some respect for my parents, at least, if not for me——'

'Because you're not likely to be home in time for breakfast, either. You see, Lacey, I keep having this fantasy about waking up in the morning with you in my arms, and making love to you before I go to work.'

Heat started to rise from the very pit of her stomach, flushing her throat and her face to embarrassed pink.

'That's very becoming,' he murmured. 'You should do it more often. So what do you suggest as an alternative, my dear? If you kept your job, once a month or so I suppose you could convince your parents that you had to check things out at the hotel, and stay overnight. But what about the rest of the time? Do you propose a series of lunch-hour rendezvous? Or meeting for cocktails, and then hurrying home for dinner so no one will wonder what else we might have been doing? No, Lacey. I'm not going to keep one eye on the clock so you can be home before curfew. You're a grown woman——'

'I'll grant it would have been easier if I was living by myself,' she admitted, 'but I don't think they'll be convinced if I suddenly announce that I'm getting an apartment of my own—especially after the Clinton closes, and I'm without a job.'

He didn't sound interested in her employment possibilities. 'It won't be necessary to go to that length to convince them. In fact, it shouldn't be hard to arrange at all.'

'I don't understand.'

He leaned forward to refill his coffee-cup. 'By tomorrow morning, Lacey, your parents will be thrilled to death that you are going to be sleeping with me.'

It had the harsh ring of truth, and it terrified her, even though she didn't understand what he meant. It hadn't exactly sounded like a threat, and yet——

'Do you mean you'd actually tell them——' Her voice gave out.

'Oh, no. I am not an idiot, Lacey. You're right, I do respect your father, and I don't think he'd agree to the trade.'

'Then how do you expect to make him think——?'

'Surely you remember there's a minor legal manoeuvre that will satisfy all their questions?' He picked up his cup and saucer and looked at her over the gold-edged rim, and said deliberately, 'It's called marriage.'

Lacey started to laugh, peals of giggles that escalated to shattering convulsions of mirth and threatened to build into hysteria.

Damon sipped his coffee and said, politely, 'You seem amused.'

She sat up suddenly uneasily aware that he didn't sound at all as if it had been a joke.

'Why?' she said baldly. 'You told me two years ago that no woman would ever own you.'

'So I did. And I haven't changed my mind. I should specify, of course, that I have no intention of this being a real marriage in more than one sense of the word. It will merely be a pro forma one, to satisfy the conventions, and allow me to have what I want, for whatever period of time I choose.'

'Me,' she said bitterly. 'I suppose I should be flattered.'

'That's up to you.' He looked at her for a long moment and said, more gently, 'Surely you didn't think I would commit myself to the Clinton without any guarantees from you, Lacey? You've done a good job tonight of explaining why you really can't be my mistress after all, except on terms you set. Well, I'm not buying it. I'm not going to be content with bits and pieces of your time, as I would have been two years ago. I'm paying too much for the privilege.'

She felt as if she'd been slapped.

'Thanks for the honour of your offer,' she said sarcastically, 'but no.'

'There's an art to compromise, you know. I sacrifice a little to get what I want, you sacrifice a little to get what you want.'

'What I used to want, perhaps,' she said bitterly. 'But no more.'

'Once you were eager to marry me, Lacey.'

'That was a long time ago. And things were very different.'

'Yes, I know. There would have been considerably more advantages for you then, wouldn't there, if you'd only been able to convince me? The sacrifice would have been mine and the freedom to dictate terms yours. Now it's a different kind of trade. I'm calling the shots this time, and I will determine when the play's over. By going through with this legal farce, I'll have you in my bed just exactly as long as I want you there, and there won't be any nasty consequences afterwards.'

She squared her shoulders. 'I won't do it.'

'Why not? It benefits you, too. You set up the rules yourself, Lacey. You'd agreed to an affair. Then you started putting limits on it. All I've done is take the limits off, and assure that we won't have to sneak around corners and be afraid of knocks at the door.'

She licked her lips nervously.

'You needn't be afraid of my holding you prisoner forever, you know.' He sounded as if he was trying to be comforting, she thought. 'The piece of paper that says we're married will be meaningless to us—it certainly won't make the affair last a single day more. I should think it would probably take a lot longer if we do it your way, as a matter of fact, with all the intrigue and the plotting. Once the fascination burns out, as it certainly will, you can get a quick divorce, and you can still hold up your head, not as Damon Kendrick's cast-aside mistress, but the wife whose story-book marriage just didn't work out.'

'Don't do this,' she whispered. 'Some day you're going to change your mind, and you'll want a normal home, a real marriage, children. Don't mess your life up like this, Damon.'

'How kind of you to have my best interests at heart,' he mocked. 'But don't fool yourself with romantic nonsense, Lacey. I decided long ago that no woman would ever control my life and that no child would ever call me Father. I haven't changed my mind in the last twenty years, and I'm not likely to in the next twenty. In any case, that's my problem, not yours. What's it going to be, Lacey? Do we surprise your parents with our happy news tonight, or do I call Bill tomorrow and tell him that I've been having second thoughts about the Clinton all along, and the fire was the final straw?'

Once, she thought, it was the culmination of my dreams to be Damon Kendrick's wife. Now it is an unspeakable thought.

Is it worse than just going to bed with him? she asked herself. You've already agreed to do that. Could it possibly be worse than the scenes you've been seeing in your head all evening, about trying to explain your conduct to your parents and your friends without telling them the horrible truth? How on earth could marriage be worse than the aftermath of an affair that it would be impossible to hide completely? Especially if Damon didn't try very hard to keep the secret...

He was right, she thought. She had set the terms herself, however unwittingly. A plastic marriage was the only way to satisfy the rules she had laid down—a plastic marriage that would, even if it had no other advantage for her, still have the supreme benefit of getting this mess behind her more quickly, because there would be no intrigue to keep him fascinated...

'All right,' she whispered unhappily.

He set his cup and saucer aside and said, 'I'll take you home.'

Her surprise must have been obvious.

'Did you think I was going to drag you back to my bedroom this instant?' he said. 'I've waited for things before, Lacey. And it's getting late; we certainly wouldn't want to cause your parents any concern, would we?'

Besides, she thought with bitter clarity, by announcing it tonight, he's taking no chances that I might think it over and find a way out—a way to change my mind.

The porch light was gleaming at the front of the Hyde Park house. It seemed to amuse Damon as he parked his Mercedes in the street. 'Did your mother call you every night in New York to tuck you in?'

'Of course not. They've probably gone to bed already.'

'I'm sure they won't mind if you wake them for such happy news.' He stopped her in the hallway the instant the front door had closed behind them. 'But before you do...'

His hands cupped her face and turned it up to his, and he feathered kisses across her cheekbone, her eyes, her nose. Then his hands slid down over her shoulder-blades and the length of her spine, holding her so firmly against his body that she began to wonder if her skin was melting from the sheer heat of his...

Only then did he turn to her mouth, gently at first, his tongue tenderly tracing the outline of her lips and then darting between, teasing, tasting...

Bill Clinton came out of the living-room, newspaper in hand. 'Lacey, Grant Collins called——' He stopped abruptly. 'Well. Hello, Damon.'

Grant, she thought hazily. He could manage the Clinton; he's got the experience. But he probably doesn't have a few million dollars in a shoe box under his bed, and without that...

Damon raised his head slowly. 'He won't be calling again.' His voice had a rough edge to it.

'Yes, I can see that,' Bill said. 'Umm—excuse me. Ginny!'

Poor Dad, Lacey thought. He's never seen anything quite like it—certainly not from Damon...

Ginny appeared in the doorway. 'Yes, dear?' Then her eyes rounded.

'In case you're wondering what you've walked into,' Damon said, 'we're going to be married next week.' He kept one arm around Lacey. It was like a strait-jacket, she thought.

Bill Clinton grinned and hugged them both. 'I'm so glad,' he confided. 'Lacey, I've always thought you and Damon belonged together.'

'So have I,' Damon said blandly.

'Next week?' Ginny's voice was a half-shriek. 'Surely you're joking? All the preparations—Lacey doesn't have a trousseau—all the things she'll need——'

'She doesn't need anything,' Damon said. 'And we're not waiting for all the wedding foolishness. We'll have a reception later, the first one in the new Clinton.'

I wanted a time limit, Lacey thought, and he's given it to me. It will certainly be over by the time the Clinton reopens, or he would have never said that. But that will be a year or more... And it might be much less, she told herself, trying to keep a smile on her face. Very likely it will be much, much less.

Tactfully, her parents withdrew so they could say a private goodnight. Lacey wondered a bit what they would have thought if they had heard the non-loverlike exchange at the front door.

'You did that on purpose,' she accused. 'Kissing me where they were sure to see! You've never done that sort of thing before.'

'No, and I probably won't again. I don't believe that making love is a spectator sport. But it seemed to convince them, didn't it? By the way, I meant it about the wedding nonsense. I won't stand for tons of orchids and miles of velvet ribbons and all that senseless trash.'

'Of course not,' Lacey said acidly. 'Though I can't imagine why you would think I wanted them. Silly trappings like that belong to a couple in love.'

He looked at her thoughtfully for a long moment before he walked back to the street and got into the Mercedes.

Damn him, she thought. He was whistling.

She had reason to remember what she'd said about the silly trappings of a couple in love the next morning when she came down to breakfast and found a single, deep crimson rose waiting by her plate. She recalled it again the morning after that, when the rose was a slighter paler red. And the day after *that*, when it was a dark pink one.

'I didn't know a young man in love still did this sort of thing,' Ginny said on the fourth day, when the florist brought a flower of such a delicate powder pink that it seemed to have been plucked from a sunset, and not a bush at all. 'Tomorrow it should be cream-coloured, and on your wedding day, it's supposed to be a pure white one, without even a trace of colour.'

'I'm sure it will be, Mother.' Lacey buried her face in the Metropolitan section of the newspaper. A young man in love, she thought in disgust. A young man putting on a good show for her parents and at the same time making sure that Lacey herself knew precisely how false each tiny, thoughtful gesture was, that was more like the truth.

'And you're not even wearing your ring,' Ginny exclaimed. 'That beautiful ring, dear...'

If I thought I could get away with it, Lacey thought, I'd drop that beautiful ring down the bathtub plug-hole. 'I'm not even dressed yet, Mother. Of course I'm not wearing it.'

'I even slept with my engagement ring on, dear. Let's go shopping, Lacey. You've been so busy at the hotel that there hasn't been time, but since it's Saturday——'

'Shopping for what, Mother?'

'I know he's got the apartment all ready, but, Lacey, surely you'd like some new underthings at least? And even if you aren't going to have bridesmaids and parties,

we could have lunch at Felicity's, just the two of us—
that's always been a special treat.'

And, because it was easier to give in than it was to
explain what Ginny would regard as the insane phenom-
enon of a bride who didn't want to shop, Lacey went
upstairs and got dressed, and put on what she had come
to think of as That Ring.

It was beautiful, she had to grant that. It was splashy,
it was stunning, and it absolutely shimmered, the central
brilliant-cut diamond and the surrounding swirl of
tapered baguettes catching and shattering even the
dimmest light into a glittering rainbow. It was the kind
of ring a girl pictured when she dreamed of her young
man slipping it on to her finger with words of love.
Lacey's had been delivered, instead, by a uniformed
special messenger from the jewellery shop, who insisted
that she sign a receipt...

Oh, yes, she thought, Damon was determined that she
didn't forget that this wasn't really going to be a marriage at all.

CHAPTER SEVEN

IT WAS the display of high-heeled, sequinned boots in the window of the Tyler-Royale department store on Country Club Plaza on Saturday that had set the flame to the fuse, but it was all Damon's fault, really, she told herself. If it hadn't been for his little games with the roses and with the diamond ring, she wouldn't have paid any attention to the boots. Instead, when Ginny pointed them out and said, 'Who on earth would wear that sort of thing?' Lacey had found herself giving the matter a great deal of thought. Damon's friend Bree of the long silver fingernails would, certainly...

She kept herself whipped into that frame of mind for the next two days. Cleaning out her office at the Clinton only added fuel to the fire; she'd scarcely had a chance to get her things settled there, and now she was leaving her job altogether. She couldn't blame him for that, exactly; she had said, after all, that she didn't want to work for him. But she had expected, at least, to keep her job until the hotel closed.

And during the endless hour of signing papers in Damon's solicitor's office—papers that protected him, it seemed to Lacey, from any circumstance, and gave her no comfort at all—she could feel the determination grow that he wasn't going to have this all his own way.

That determination even helped to keep her head high during the brief and to-the-point ceremony on Monday evening in the judge's chambers, and it carried her through the celebration dinner afterwards with her parents. It was safer, at least, than thinking about what was happening to her...

It wasn't until much later, when she was alone for the moment in Damon's bedroom, that she began to have doubts about what she had planned. But it was too late for that, she told herself, and before she could talk herself out of it, she dumped the contents of her overnight bag out on the polished top of a bureau. He had tactfully suggested that she might like to have a few minutes alone, but she couldn't count on him being patient for long. And there was such a lot to be done...

She swore under her breath when she realised that she'd bought a kit of false fingernails that didn't include any glue. 'I'll bet this sort of thing never happens to Bree,' she muttered. Well, it was simply lack of experience—I'll learn, she thought with a shrug. In the meantime, I'll just have to improvise.

So she lavishly spread adhesive from the tube that had come with the false eyelashes on to the inch-long gold fingernails and applied them with care. A beauty spot on her left cheek, some vibrant lipstick in a shade half-way between magenta and fuchsia, and the eyelashes, so long that they tickled whenever she blinked.

The combination looked a little odd against the background of the ivory designer dress she had worn to that meaningless ceremony in the courthouse, so she hung the dress up carefully in the almost-empty side of the wardrobe and kept one eye on the door as she slid hastily into the outfit she had so carefully chosen for this night...

My wedding night, she thought. How different it is from what I once hoped for.

Stop it, she told herself firmly. You can't change what is; you have to live with it.

She dragged her attention back to the make-up case. A little more eyeliner, perhaps? Oh, and she'd forgotten the bubble gum...

She didn't hear the door open. She was peering into the mirror that topped his bureau, applying a little more mascara to the tips of the false eyelashes and thinking that he really ought to be considerate enough to put a dressing-table in his bedroom if he was going to have female company. At the sound of his voice she straightened up very suddenly, accidentally jabbing the brush into the corner of her eye, and mascara and tears streamed down across her face.

'What in the hell are you doing?' Damon said. He sounded stunned.

She turned around, slowly, to face him. She mopped the mascara off her cheek with a tissue and slowly and deliberately blew an enormous bubble with her wad of gum. Then she said, 'I'm making sure neither of us forgets what's really going on here tonight.'

He rubbed his jaw with the back of his hand and finally said, 'I see. Would you turn around, please? All the way around?'

She did, slowly. She almost lost her balance, once; the heels of her ankle-high gold-sequinned boots were more compatible with hard pavements than with deep plush carpeting. And worse than her own awkwardness was the intensity with which he was studying her, from the toes of her boots to the top of her teased hair, lingering especially on the abbreviated hem of her leather skirt and the ruffled black organdie blouse, which made perfectly plain the fact that she was wearing nothing underneath.

Then he threw himself down in an armchair and laughed until he had to pull out a handkerchief and mop tears from his eyes.

Lacey put her hands on her hips, which only made her skirt shorter, and said, 'It's not supposed to be funny!'

'You should see it from here.' It was an unrepentant murmur. 'I assure you——'

'Laughter was not the reaction I was hoping for.'

'Oh?' It was silky. He stood up, pulled off his tie, and draped it over the arm of the chair. 'Would you rather have this one?' He advanced on her slowly, unbuttoning his shirt.

She backed away, and her stiletto heels tangled in the carpet, throwing her off balance. Damon caught her and flung her down on the big bed. He started to unbutton the delicate buttons, his hand warm against her skin. 'Damn buttons,' he muttered. 'There must be a hundred of them. Not such a good choice, after all, intriguing though it is.' Impatience won out, and he bent his head to her breast, licking her nipple through the flimsy fabric, then drawing it into his mouth to caress it slowly. His hand rested gently on her knee for an instant, and then began to move slowly up her thigh, under the leather skirt. A shockingly strong wave of desire seemed to arc through her like an electrical current, and Lacey moaned, and then choked, gasped, and started to cough.

Damon acted instantly, pulling her up to a sitting position cradled against his chest, and patting her back. 'What happened?' he asked when she was breathing easily again.

'I swallowed my gum,' she admitted reluctantly. 'And don't snigger at me.'

'I understand, dear. You're horribly disappointed in me, aren't you? You thought when it came right down to it that I'd be revolted by the image of you as a street-walker. Well, you're partly right; actually, I would rather kiss you instead of the half-inch of goop you're wearing. Shall we go wash your face, and take the black widow spiders off your eyes?'

Miserably, she let him lead her into the bathroom and scrub the make-up off, and she didn't even fuss when he dropped the false eyelashes into the wastebasket. The darn things itched; she wondered how any woman ever managed to adjust herself to wearing them all the time.

'I'm surprised your towels aren't monogrammed,' she said spitefully as he rinsed out the flannel and started again.

One dark eyebrow lifted. 'With what? *His* and *Hers*?'

'Not at all. *His* and—*Next*, I should think, or *For Whom It May Concern.*'

He grinned. 'Be careful about what you say, or you might—accidentally, of course—get soap in your mouth. Are you feeling jealous of whoever might follow you, Lacey?'

'I am not——'

'Don't be. If you keep up this sort of thing, you'll last a good long time.' He dried her face with a thick towel and kissed the tip of her nose. 'That's much better. And as soon as we get you out of those dress-up clothes——'

'You actually don't care how I feel about this?' she said quietly. 'You honestly wouldn't rather have a willing woman than one you've blackmailed into your bed?'

His fingertips returned to the half-undone buttons of her blouse and began a steady downward progress, over the quick rise and fall of her breasts, until the organdie was no longer a barricade. His hands slid under the delicate fabric and spanned the sides of her waist, his thumbs caressing the soft tips of her breasts until they were eager peaks.

'What's your definition of willing?' he asked huskily. 'You keep telling me you don't want to be here, but your body has a language all its own, my dear.'

When he took her back into the bedroom, she did not resist. She tried very hard, instead, to detach herself from what he was doing to her, the sensations he was arousing as he undressed her slowly and carefully.

You can't stop him, she told herself, but you don't have to co-operate.

He knelt to pull off the gold-sequinned boots, and held one up for a closer inspection before setting it aside with a half-smile. Then he cupped his hand around the high arch of her foot and raised it; she had to clutch at his shoulder to keep her balance. 'You've got such tiny feet,' he said huskily, and kissed her toes. She shivered and tried to pull away from him. 'And such beautiful legs...' His hand slipped gently up her thigh and released her sheer black stockings from the garter. Every inch of skin he touched seemed to explode into flame as with both hands he rolled the stocking down over her knee, over her ankle. Finally he flung it aside and reached for the top of the other stocking.

She writhed under his touch. 'Please,' she said, 'just finish it. Don't torment me like this.'

'Lacey, I've waited two and a half years for this night,' he whispered. 'I'm not going to be satisfied with passive acceptance.'

Then I'll fight him, she told herself. But I will not feed his ego by responding to him. He'll have to force me...

He unfastened the soft leather skirt and eased it down, his hands warm against the curve of her hips. The last scrap of lace was quickly disposed of, and he sat back on his heels and looked up at her for a long moment, harsh desire lighting his face, before he rose and reached for her.

She ducked away from his hands and slid under the blankets, her head turned away. He laughed softly and a moment later joined her there, the quick heat of his naked body searing her delicate skin as he drew her close.

He did not use force. He used instead the power of her own mind, and he seemed to know intuitively how best to fan to white heat the erotic sensations that lay so thinly concealed inside her. She clutched the edges of a pillow, and gritted her teeth, and he bent his head to nibble once more at her breast.

His fingertips quested gently to the most sensitive, secret spots of her being, feeding a pulsating, throbbing hunger deep inside her, and, when he withdrew that gentle touch without satisfying the longing, she could stand no more. She cried out, an incoherent sound that might have been his name, and arched against him, pulling him down to her, no longer caring that she was granting him a victory she had sworn to withhold.

Triumph flared in his eyes at her surrender, and with a hoarse little moan he moved above her, and invaded her body with his own.

There was a tiny instant of discomfort—more of surprise than of pain—and then the pulsing beat of desire began to slowly build again as he moved inside her, rising to a level that threatened to rip her apart. She clung frantically to him, pleading, begging, as his control snapped and the waves of sensation threatened to consume them both, and still she held on, as the world shattered around her and in the same single instant Damon gave a harsh cry and collapsed against her, panting and dishevelled.

She caught herself just as she reached to stroke his sweat-dampened hair back from his brow, and stopped in mid-motion. The warm weight of him held her prisoner just as effectively as his passion had; he turned his head and pressed his lips against her temple, and it was like a brand resting on her skin. He was not going to let her forget how completely he had possessed her, she thought, how absolutely he had humbled her, and how unconditionally he had forced her surrender.

'Please,' she said, in a soft little whisper, and he raised his head.

'That was what you call unwilling?' he murmured.

It stung. 'If your lust is quite satisfied, Damon——'

He smiled. 'I'm afraid so, for the moment.' He slipped away from her, as if reluctant to leave the soft comfort of her body.

She hadn't expected to feel cold, but the room air hitting her overheated skin, combined with the quizzical way he was looking at her, sent a convulsed shiver over her, and she reached for the blankets he had flung aside.

Damon captured her hand. 'No hiding,' he said. His fingertips traced the soft marks on her breasts where his chest hair had rubbed her delicate skin to redness. 'Let me look at you.'

'You're sadistic.'

'Did I hurt you?' It was soft, and he was apparently so certain of the answer that he sounded unconcerned.

She bit her tongue. 'Not exactly,' she said reluctantly.

He raised up on one elbow. 'Did I do anything to you that you didn't want me to do?'

She wouldn't look at him.

'No,' he answered his own question. 'I didn't. So what are you complaining about? The fact that I made you feel like a woman?'

She turned her back to him, but she couldn't avoid that soft, persistent voice.

'That was the first time for you, wasn't it?' he said.

'I suppose you're proud of the fact!'

'Very.' He slipped an arm gently around her and pulled her back against him until she lay cradled against his chest with his arm possessively under her breasts. 'To be your first lover,' he murmured into her ear, 'and to know that every man you sleep with for all your life will be measured against me—yes, I'm pleased.'

As if, she thought, he believes I'll end up just like him—going from one lover to the next, each relationship the perfect one for a moment, or a week or a month... She shuddered at the thought.

'Don't be ashamed of what you felt, Lacey.'

She struck out at him. 'I felt abused. And battered. And——'

He moved suddenly, and she found herself on her back, pinned to the bed by the weight of his body. 'In that case,' he said grimly, 'there's no reason for me to waste time on gentleness in the future, is there? If you feel that what happened between us a few minutes ago was rape, then I might as well take what I want without concern for you, whenever I feel the urge.'

Her breath seemed to freeze in her throat. His hands were roaming her body, roughly plundering, slipping under her to rearrange her to accommodate him. There was no doubt that he was feeling that urge right now, and she panicked and said, in a voice that cracked, 'No, Damon—please, no——'

'Was it so awful, Lacey?' he demanded.

'No,' she breathed. 'Not exactly.'

His hands gentled, and he whispered, 'Don't lie to me about this, Lacey. You're going to belong to me body and soul, for as long as I want you. And when we're finished, and you take another lover, you'll be able to teach him a few things about how to make love to you— things that you've learned from me.'

'No,' she said, but the fire had started to build again under the seeking mastery of his touch, and as before there was no banking it into oblivion, and no time to think about exactly what it was that she had been trying to deny...

He looked like a sleeping angel in the half-light that filtered through the curtains over the long glass doors that led out on to the balcony. She looked at him a little suspiciously; was he really asleep? She had a vague feeling that she had been thoroughly stroked, not so long ago, as if she were a kitten, and that she had responded as a kitten might have. But it must have been only a guilty dream, for Damon released a long sigh that wasn't quite a snore, and rolled on to his back.

His face was wiped clean of all emotion, save perhaps contentment. Long dark lashes lay heavily against his cheekbones, and in his hair, which was a rumpled mass of dark curls, a single long gold fingernail glistened in the light of a stray sunbeam.

Lacey held up her hands and sighed. She could account for a grand total of four nails at the moment, counting the one in Damon's hair. What had happened to the other six was beyond her, but it was obvious that false-eyelash adhesive wasn't going to catch on as a substitute glue.

Damn, she thought. Everything I tried to accomplish last night went wrong. I'll bet Bree never loses a nail, no matter how rumbustious things get in bed.

And don't forget it for an instant, she told herself. Because when you're gone, Bree—or someone just like her—will take your place.

And why that should give her a fluttery, empty feeling in the pit of her stomach was beyond her. It's anticipation, she told herself, and the hope that it won't take too long. That's all.

'Good morning.' Damon's voice was soft and lazy and low. He traced her profile with a careless finger, and then leaned over her to take a long, deep kiss, his tongue teasing against hers and then playfully tracing the outline of her mouth.

Lacey tried to hold herself rigid, but within a minute her insides had curled up into tight little knots of anticipation. Dammit, she thought, it isn't fair that my body betrays me, too!

'You're not talking this morning?' he asked softly. 'That's all right. There are other ways to greet the day, and your lover.' His hand rested gently on her knee for a moment and then moved slowly, enticingly, upwards. 'I've dreamed about this, Lacey. Holding you like this, and making love to you——'

She sighed and turned her head aside. Why even try to fight him? she thought. He had already stripped her of her pride; what else could he take? Let him do what he wanted; he would, anyway.

'No, Lacey,' he murmured, 'you can't pretend you're not here. And I'm not going to give you a chance to pretend that I'm not.'

She could not suppress a little moan as he took her; there was no pain, just a feeling of inevitability as the tiny flames of desire began to lick at her body, slowly rising in intensity and turning her eventually into a raging, writhing creature who was almost screaming as she pleaded for release from this tormenting ecstasy—a release Damon was only too happy to provide...

Afterwards he cradled her when she burst into sobs, half in shame, half in embarrassment at the frenzied way she had responded to him. He pressed a line of gentle kisses the length of her throat: warm, tender caresses. 'Don't be frightened,' he whispered. 'It's an emotionally jarring experience, and it's scared you, that's all. You've got a lovely sensual nature, my dear, and as soon as you learn to accept yourself——'

Which only made her cry harder. How could I have done that? she asked herself hopelessly. How could I have let myself respond to him like that?

When she had exhausted her tears, he tucked the blankets gently around her and held her till she went to sleep again.

The sun was high when she woke, and he was gone. For a moment, as she stretched catlike, she felt wonderfully rested and happy. Then her hand encountered the sharp edge of one of the missing false fingernails loose among the tangled sheets, and she flung herself out of the bed as if the hounds of death were pursuing her—or as if Damon might be waiting just outside the door.

She made the bed up with quick, rough motions, pulling the sheets and blankets tight. Humphrey might be too much the gentleman's gentleman to snigger, she thought, or he might have seen this sort of thing too often to care, but she still would rather straighten out the jumbled mess herself.

And as for her play-acting props from last night— Damon must have felt somewhat the same way, she thought, when she found her organdie blouse neatly folded in the corner of a drawer, with the toe of a se-quinned boot glittering underneath.

It was pretty foolish, she thought, to believe that I could actually embarrass him.

She gathered up the scattered gold fingernails and stood biting her lip when she could only find nine of them. As it was, she'd had to hunt for the ninth one, and had finally found it in a slipper, pushed under the edge of the bed.

She gave up on it, finally, and went to take a shower. It ought to be amusing if the missing fingernail was still in Damon's hair, she thought. It could have quite an effect on a board of directors' meeting, for instance...

Humphrey was pouring coffee into a china cup at the very instant she entered the dining-room, and Lacey stopped in the doorway for an instant in surprise. How had he known precisely when she would walk in? 'Good morning, Mrs Kendrick,' he said, in a gently respectful tone, and held her chair.

Mrs Kendrick, she thought. And to think that once I wanted that title so much, I'd have done nearly anything to get it.

'What may I get you for breakfast?' Humphrey asked.

She refused anything but the coffee and hoped that he would just go away, but he hovered a bit nervously, and she finally pushed the cup aside and asked as pleasantly as she could what he wanted. He began to tell her what he'd planned to serve for dinner that night, and she nodded briskly and told him it sounded fine to her. 'In fact,' she added, 'you do such a splendid job of running Mr Kendrick's household that I wouldn't dream of interfering. So there's really no need to check these things out with me. Just carry on as you always have.'

She dismissed him with a smile and went straight to the front door. The place was going to smother her if she had to spend two more minutes in it, that was certain.

She was almost to the lobby before she realised what had been missing this morning. There had not been a red rose on her pillow, or a note, or a personal message of any sort.

'So much for the silly trappings,' she muttered. 'Damon obviously feels we've got past the need for those.' She looked gloomily at the diamond starburst on her left hand, snuggled up next to the carved band he'd placed there yesterday in the judge's chambers, and shuddered. Just how long would this farce continue?

She spent the day window-shopping; although the things she'd signed at the solicitor's office yesterday had included the paperwork for a new bank account, she got cold shivers at the idea of using it. It made it so horribly plain that she was being paid for her presence in Damon's bed. Especially, she thought, when it was so apparent that there was nothing else she would be useful for in that elegant apartment. Between them, Damon and Humphrey had everything under perfect contol.

Especially me, she thought . . .

* * *

She stopped at the Clinton late that afternoon, just to see what was going on, when she saw the vans parked under the front canopy. One bore the name of a steam-cleaning company. Already, she saw, the lobby carpets had nearly regained their original glow, as if there had never been a fire. She stepped carefully over the big vacuum hoses and walked across to the door of the coffee-shop, where two electricians were busy in the kitchen, and a carpenter was sizing up the damage to the restaurant area. Nearby, Bill Clinton was leaning against a pillar listening intently to Grant Collins.

And just what was Grant doing here? Lacey wondered. Her father spotted her and waved, and Grant turned. She could feel the cold disapproval in his glance as she crossed the room to meet them.

'Lacey!' Her father gave her an affectionate hug. 'Looks pretty good, doesn't it? They've finished cleaning all the rooms upstairs, too.'

'I thought perhaps you weren't going to bother.'

'Well, it'll take a few weeks to get the work really rolling, and Damon's going to keep the place open while they work on the top few floors. Might as well keep some money coming in as long as possible.'

'I see. Hello, Grant.'

'Mrs Kendrick.' The words had a cynical little twist.

'I guess Damon hasn't had a chance to tell you the details,' Bill Clinton said with a grin. 'Grant's going to help out for a while—get the place in the habit of running Hoteliers-style.'

The carpenter called, 'Mr Clinton? You want panelling on this wall, too?'

Bill Clinton went over to talk to him.

'You're going to manage this place behind the scenes? On top of your regular job?' Lacey asked. 'That will be quite a load, won't it, Grant?'

'Mr Kendrick seemed to think I'll have time on my hands.' He sounded a little bitter.

She bit her lip.

He added crossly. 'I'll consider myself lucky if the only consequence is working seventy-hour weeks for a while. He could have transferred me to the hotel he owns in Juneau, Alaska, as head caretaker!'

'Grant, really——'

'Dammit, Lacey, why did you lie to me? You told me there was nothing going on between you and Damon Kendrick. If I'd had any idea what I was messing around with, I would never——' He seemed to realise that he wasn't being very flattering, and he shot a sideways look at her. 'Talk about ruining my chances for job security!'

'It won't. I promise you that.'

'Listen, do me a favour and don't try to be helpful, all right? I'd just as soon not call any more attention to myself.'

He walked away, fast, as if he didn't even want to be seen talking to her. Lacey sighed. She couldn't exactly blame him. From Grant's point of view, it must look as if she'd stirred up his career trouble for the sheer fun of meddling.

She waved at her father, who was still deep in conversation with the carpenter, and walked slowly back to the Kendrick Kansas City.

I think I'm losing my mind, she thought. After the encounter with Grant, the penthouse actually looked like a haven of peace...

That illusion, however, lasted only as long as it took to get inside. From the door she could see the back of a dark head in a chair in the living-room. She glanced at her wristwatch and swore under her breath. What was Damon doing home at this hour? She'd had the impression that he never left his office before six.

'Hello, Damon,' she said, determined to put the best possible face on it.

The dark head turned, and a pair of brown eyes studied her with interest. Then the man in the chair rose. 'I'm not Damon,' he said. 'And you're certainly not Damon's usual. So let's have a drink while you tell me about yourself, darling.'

CHAPTER EIGHT

HUMPHREY came hurriedly through the living-room. 'Mrs Kendrick, I——'

'Mrs *who*?' The man wheeled around to stare at her. 'Damon actually got married? And without telling his little brother, too. Well, I'd say that calls for a bit of an explanation.'

Little brother? Of course, she thought in relief as things settled back into place in her brain. She'd never met Dirk Kendrick, who seemed to divide his time equally between the Riviera, Palm Beach and a yacht in the Caribbean, but she'd heard about him. Not from Damon, however. The stray bits of information that had come her way about Dirk had been mostly gleaned from the society section of the *Sunday Star*.

'And it calls for a little celebration, too. Humphrey, get the lady a drink.'

Humphrey's eyes met Lacey's with a sort of regretful frustration, like the look of a puppy who was afraid he was in trouble. She smiled and nodded, and Humphrey brought her a glass of wine and then freshened Dirk's drink. It was apparently not his first, Lacey thought. She took a chair opposite him.

'Just wait till I see him,' Dirk said. 'All that self-righteous talk of his about never getting married, and now he's run his head into the noose, after all. Not that you aren't a very nice-looking noose,' he added hastily. 'But he should have asked me. I'd have told him, it isn't worth it. Been married three times myself; I ought to know.'

Lacey sipped her wine and thought about it. Was Dirk's experience why Damon was so set against the idea of marriage? Married three times, obviously without success; it would give anyone qualms.

'But then you are a lot different from his usual,' Dirk admitted handsomely.

'Thank you.' Lacey's voice was crisp. 'I'm flattered.'

He frowned and thought it over. 'That didn't come out quite right, did it?' he confided. 'All three of my ex-wives said I never had any tact. Maybe we'd better talk about something else instead.'

Lacey laughed. His version of the Kendrick charm was certainly different from Damon's, but it was there, none the less.

'The weather? Too blasted hot in this city, that's all I've got to say about it. I know, we can talk about art—that's safe,' Dirk said. 'Though I don't pretend to understand Damon's taste. Take that, for instance——' he waved his glass towards the fireplace '—it looks just like a boot to me.'

Lacey turned her head so fast that her neck snapped. Sure enough, there on the end of the mantel, in pristine glory, sat a gold-sequinned boot.

It can't be, she thought. I saw those boots this morning in a drawer in the bedroom.

Or had she? She had certainly seen one glittering toe, but had there been a pair?

In any case, it didn't matter a bit now. However it had got from the bedroom to the mantel, it was certainly her boot, flamingly out of place in this tastefully quiet room, displayed—no, flaunted!—for all the world to see.

I'll kill him, she decided.

'Actually, I find it a fascinating piece of sculpture,' Damon said blandly from the doorway. He gave Lacey a half-smile and came into the room. 'Hello, Dirk. What brings you back to Kansas City?'

'It's been a while since I heard from you. Now I find out why.' Dirk rose to shake his brother's hand.

For an instant, as they faced each other, they looked enough alike to be twins. Damon was an inch taller; Dirk carried considerably more weight around the waist, and his face had a ruddier cast. Take the glass out of his hand for a few months, Lacey thought, and he'd probably end up the mirror image of his brother.

Dirk jerked his head towards Lacey. 'You could have told me about this.'

Damon shrugged. He poured himself a glass of wine and sat down on the arm of Lacey's chair, his hand resting casually on the nape of her neck, under her hair. 'It was sort of a sudden thing.'

'So were my first two,' Dirk confided. 'Disaster—sheer disaster. I leaped before I looked, and——'

'And the last one was no better,' Damon said. 'Shall we let the ladies in your past rest in peace, Dirk? It's hardly tasteful to discuss your many divorces, under the circumstances.'

'Oh, right. We'll go back to talking about art.' He squinted at the boot. 'Who perpetrated that thing, anyway?'

'I doubt you'd know the name,' Damon said smoothly. 'I believe the—artist—is Italian.'

'He certainly should have been—that pair of boots cost enough,' Lacey muttered. 'What are you going to do with the other one? Plant flowers in it and put it on the balcony?'

Amusement glinted in Damon's eyes. 'Would you like to go and freshen up before dinner, Dirk? Humphrey's arranged for you to have a suite on the next floor down.'

Lacey moved uneasily under the slow, erotic circles his thumb were drawing on the soft skin at the back of her neck.

'What's the matter?' Dirk asked suspiciously. 'Have you already turned that guest bedroom into a nursery?'

Damon was smiling down at her. He didn't seem to notice the jab. 'Having on several occasions been a newly-wed yourself,' he murmured, 'surely you understand that there's a natural desire for privacy?'

'Oh. Well, I can take a hint.'

Damon waited till he was out of the room, and said, 'But only if it's attached to a brick, and applied over his head.' He put a finger under Lacey's chin to raise her face to his and kissed her, long and lazily. 'What have you been doing today?'

'Shopping.'

'Oh, good. Does that mean I have something even more exotic than last night to look forward to?'

Exotic. Well, she couldn't exactly blame him for seeing it that way; she had certainly asked for it.

He pulled her out of the chair and into his arms. His hand slid down her spine with slow sensuality, holding her against the hard length of him with ease. 'I've been thinking about you all day,' he whispered. 'The scent of you, the feel of you, and the way you looked last night, as I made love to you——'

She was having a little trouble breathing. It's fear, she thought, fear that things will be no different tonight. And if I lose control of myself again tonight——

She kept her voice even and casual. 'If that's the case, your secretary must have appreciated having an easier day than usual.'

He shook his head. 'Tougher, because I'd much rather have been here with you. Oh, the hell with it, my sweet Lacey, let's go to bed.'

'You have a guest.' She tried not to sound too relieved.

'Damn Dirk,' he said huskily. 'I certainly didn't invite him. And in any case, Dirk's a good example of the reason we went through that silly ceremony yesterday.

Honeymooners are forgiven lots of things, including the insatiable desire to be alone together.'

'Despite his ill-luck,' she said evenly, 'it sounds as if Dirk has a great deal more respect for the institution of marriage than you do.'

'Of course he does.' He sounded surprised that she had thought it worth a comment. 'Dirk's the perpetual optimist. He's always looking for the silver lining in every cloud, and the pot of gold at the base of every rainbow.'

'While you are the cynic.'

'The realist,' he corrected. 'His ex-wives are living in comfort in various spots around the world, courtesy of quite generous alimony——'

'While your ex-wife,' she began, 'will——'

He frowned. 'You're a long way from being my ex-anything, Lacey.' He kissed her, hard, as if to prove his point.

You shouldn't have got your hopes up, she told herself. You ought to know better than to let yourself think that last night might have satisfied him, that by today he'd be starting to look for other games to play.

Humphrey came in just then to ask about the wines for dinner, and she slipped away from Damon with a tiny suppressed sigh of relief. He let her go easily enough, but the way he looked at her made it apparent that while she might have won a delay, the final reckoning would be his, and the glow in his eyes promised that he would not be patient for long.

Dirk settled himself on a loveseat in the living-room with an expansive sigh. 'Humphrey, you outdid yourself,' he said simply. 'Never mind the coffee, Lacey. I don't want to lose the glorious taste of that Grand Marnier soufflé.'

Humphrey allowed himself a small smile as he set the coffee-tray on the centre table. Lacey took the chair across from Dirk and reached for a cup and saucer. 'Will you take Mr Kendrick's coffee to him in the library, Humphrey?' she asked. 'I'm sure if his telephone calls take long, he'll appreciate it.'

And it might encourage him to talk longer, too, she thought. Which would be a relief of a sort; at least when he wasn't in the room, he couldn't look at her as he had all the way through dinner—sort of as if he was a child with his nose pressed to a candy-store window, and she was an entire jar of chocolate-covered peanuts...

'He's still working as hard as ever?' Dirk said. 'I never understood that, you know. Sure, the corporation pays him a nice salary on top of his stockholder's benefits, but it's not as if he has to work. And the boy just keeps taking on more. This latest hotel he's bought, for instance. It's going to be more trouble than it's worth. He should have learned his lesson from this one.'

'I think the Kendrick's beautiful.' Lacey wasn't stupid; she'd heard Damon firmly change the subject when Dirk asked about the Clinton, and she wasn't about to get herself involved.

'Oh, beautiful, yes. But worth it?' He shook his head. 'Not that I bother with the arithmetic—as long as I get my dividends every quarter, I don't care what else happens in the Hoteliers offices.' He leaned back in his chair. 'Not for me the life of a corporate slave,' he added contentedly. 'I like being in charge of my own time, not having to answer to anyone else.'

'Damon doesn't answer to anyone,' she said mildly. 'He's the one everyone answers to.' She stirred a little cream into her coffee.

Dirk laughed. 'In the long run, being the boss only means that you're at everyone's beck and call. Running around the country putting out fires, trying to stay ahead of the competition, that's not for me. I'd rather call myself a free man—swim and play tennis and dance till dawn——'

And what do you have to show for it, Lacey wondered, except three alimony bills every month?

'How about you?' he asked. He leaned forwards and his hand brushed her knee—accidentally, she thought. Surely it must have been accidental? 'Lacey, how long are you going to be happy waiting around for that dull dog to get off the telephone or out of the office and do something worthwhile?'

'I hardly think——'

'That this is a fit subject for us to talk about?' He chuckled. 'Well, I take my opportunities where I find them, and if I'd seen you first, Damon would have been out of luck.'

The soft pressure of his hand on her knee was nothing compared to the iron band that seemed to be tightening around her heart. As if I would have chosen you over him, Dirk! she thought icily.

'So I can't feel too badly about taking advantage of opportunity when it knocks,' he went on smoothly. 'If Damon weren't such a fool, he'd know better than to trust his lovely lady alone in a room with any man.'

'Even his brother,' she said bitterly.

'Oh, especially his brother,' Dirk confided. 'I've got all the Kendrick advantages, you see, without that overdeveloped sense of responsibility that Damon acquired—where, I'll never know. I got the lucky genes, I guess you could say.'

Lazy ones would be a better way to put it, she thought icily. Dirk Kendrick was a parasite. Too lazy to work, he took from the corporation without thought of contributing to it. Too lazy even to find a woman for himself, he was trying to take from the brother whose guest he was. It was enough to make her feel sick.

She removed his hand from her knee and placed it with cold precision on the arm of his chair. 'If you touch me again,' she warned, 'you will find out how it feels to take a shower in hot coffee. That goes for now, next month, and fifty years in the future, because I am not interested in your sleazy proposition, Dirk.'

'Sleazy?' he protested. 'All I said was, when you get tired of waiting around for him, I'd be more than happy——'

'How in the hell can you think that any woman who loves Damon could possibly consider——' She stopped, as suddenly as if her vocal cords had been cut.

Love? Oh, surely not, she thought distractedly. It was only something I said half-consciously, to make my point with this arrogant idiot!

But were not the facts that sprang from the half-conscious mind the truest ones of all?

I loved him once, that's true, she thought. But I got over that when I discovered that he didn't love me. And I cannot possibly love anyone who is only using me for his own pleasure, she told herself frantically. Someone who is capable of forcing me into the situation I'm in now.

Force? Had it truly been a matter of force?

He had offered her an unpalatable choice, that was true. But she could have refused it. Her parents would have been hurt and horrified, and that would have been the end of the sale. But they would not have blamed her for rejecting such an insulting proposal. They would simply have worked out something else.

So, why hadn't she rejected it?

'Why haven't you told Bill about my indecent offer?' Damon had asked once. At the time, she had still been making the excuse to herself that she had kept silent because she hadn't wanted to hurt her father, to destroy his liking for his young colleague. And, she had told herself at the time, she was certain that, no matter what Damon said, he did want the Clinton, and if she was to tell Bill the truth it would destroy the chance of making a deal at any time. But it had been more than that. Oh, so much more.

You wanted him all along, Lacey, she told herself. No matter what the terms, no matter what the conditions.

She could see it now, as clearly as if a sluice of cold rain had washed away the fog in which she had wandered around for so long. Love wasn't something that could be given only to someone who deserved it, or who promised to return it in kind. The truth was that she had never stopped loving him.

Damon had been right all along. She wanted him, every bit as badly as he wanted her, and that was why she had not been able to reject him last night. To reject him would have been to tear herself apart as well . . .

Dirk said, 'Good lord, you really do love him, don't you?'

She nodded.

There was a long silence, and then he said awkwardly, 'I'm sorry, Lacey. I guess I've never realised that there really could be a woman like you. Damon's a lucky dog.'

She closed her eyes against the pain that his clumsy sympathy had caused. I certainly can't stand to talk about it, she thought. I should never have admitted it to him, no matter what. 'Would you like coffee now, Dirk?'

'Huh? Oh, sure.'

With determination she turned the conversation to the places where he lived, and when Damon came back they were talking easily once more. Dirk didn't stay long after that. 'I know you need your rest, Damon,' he said with heavy-handed humour. 'All these responsibilities you've taken on. I suppose the next time I come you'll have started a family, too, and acquired a dog and a house in Mission Hills. Well, each to his own. I'm leaving tomorrow for Europe, by the way.' He gestured at the boot. 'If I get into Italy, I'll look up your sculptor friend and send you the mate to that for a wedding present.'

Damon closed the door behind him and leaned against it, laughing. 'Poor Dirk,' he said. 'No tact, and an incredible ability to believe in the miraculous.'

Lacey picked up the empty cups and set them back on the coffee-tray. 'Such as?' she said quietly.

'Happy marriages. Kids. Dogs. Houses in the suburbs. He doesn't want any of those things himself any more than I do, but it comforts him to believe in them.'

'It would seem only likely that some day you'll want to pass all this on.' She hated herself for saying it.

'To whom? Someone just like Dirk? Business heads don't always run in families, Lacey. And I can't think of anything I'd less like to discuss tonight than the future of the corporation, anyway.' He reached for her.

'Why did you put that boot on the mantel, Damon?'

'Isn't that the best place to keep trophies?' he asked blandly. 'And now that we are finally alone, my sweet Lacey...'

A trophy. That was all she was to him. A beautiful object to use, to admire, to show off, until the pride of ownership, the triumph of the victory, wore off. And then, what? Would he try to banish her, to keep her out of sight?

It reminded her of something, vaguely, and then she remembered Grant Collins, and his fear of being sent to the far corner of the globe. 'I talked to Grant today,' she said.

Damon sighed. 'Is this important?'

'It is to him. He's very concerned that he will lose his job at the Kendrick because of me. Because of——' She intended to say, *this affair of ours*. Instead, she said, very softly, 'Because of us.'

His eyes narrowed. 'Was there anything going on between you and Grant?'

He had misinterpreted that last husky word, she realised. 'No,' she said tartly. 'And you don't need to be concerned about the future, either.' She stopped herself; how close she had come to telling him that he didn't need to worry about her loyalty! Instead, she said, 'You terrified him—as a matter of fact, he didn't even want to be seen talking to me today.'

He looked down at her for a long moment. 'Don't worry,' he drawled. 'I doubt that I scared him off permanently—he'll still be around when you want him.'

She wanted to scream that she didn't want Grant Collins, that she would never under any circumstances want him. She wanted to strike out at Damon, to bruise that handsome face with her fists until he admitted that she had a right to have feelings, too. Or, failing that, she wanted to huddle in his arms and cry, and plead with him to love her as she loved him... And that was the most frightening option of all.

'But until then,' Damon said, 'I don't think we'll have any trouble keeping your mind off him.'

His hands came to rest familiarly on her hips, holding her taut against him, and his mouth claimed hers with slow, sensual mastery.

How, she asked herself despairingly, am I going to survive this? How am I going to exist, balancing my love for him with the knowledge that he does not think of me as anything more than an intriguing bed partner, for a while?

She could scarcely breathe; he had kissed her until nothing about her was working quite right any more. Certainly her voice shouldn't sound like a stiff little whisper, but it did.

'Damon, how long do you plan to leave that boot on the mantel?'

He raised his head and looked at it, glittering in the indirect light. 'Damn the boot,' he said. 'It's an interesting curiosity, that's all.'

In its own way, she thought, that was the harshest blow of all. She was nothing more than an *interesting curiosity*, was she?

He picked her up and carried her into the bedroom. 'Costumes are all very well,' he said huskily as he undressed her, 'but this is the way I was picturing you today, at the most inappropriate moments...' She trembled under his touch, and he smiled and scooped her off her feet and into the big bed.

This is a farce, she thought, as his caresses grew more ardent. It's a fraud, just the image of love without a fragment of substance.

But she could not deny the way her body was responding almost automatically to the demands of his. His breathing was rough and rasping, his body was urgent against her softness, until the last barricade of her self-defence crumbled into dust.

If the image is all I can have, she thought half-coherently, then for tonight it will have to be enough.

And she closed her eyes to the consequences, and flung herself into a maelstrom that left her spent and shaking and clinging to him...

He fell asleep much later with his head on her shoulder, his breath warm against her delicate skin, one hand curved casually around her breast. And for what was possibly the longest hour of her life Lacey lay there and watched him sleep, imprisoned by his weight, and by the burden of her own thoughts.

I should simply leave, she thought, while I still have some dignity. It would be fitting, after all, to destroy his pride by publicly walking out on him; he had certainly destroyed hers. Not in the way he had intended, perhaps, but just as surely.

You will belong to me body and soul, he had said, and she knew now how true it was, how true it would always be. It had been distressing enough last night to admit that he had the power to awaken a sensual self she had not known existed. But tonight, when she had discovered how much more it was possible to want him, need him, love him——

And, if he ever came to suspect that, she knew she would never be able to hold up her head again.

Leave, she told herself quietly. Just gather your things together and leave. After all, what could he do? The papers had been signed for the Clinton's purchase. If he tried to back out of that, he would have to admit to the bargain they had struck, and surely he would not do that? He would accept the inevitable, and, knowing Damon, he would probably laugh at the idea of being beaten at his own game.

But the idea of walking away made her want to curl up and die inside. To be without him altogether would be even worse than this travesty of a marriage, and she was too weak to turn her back just now.

Tomorrow, she thought. I might be strong enough tomorrow.

She stopped in surprise at the door of the dining-room the next morning, and her eyes went to her wristwatch. Surely it couldn't be so badly wrong as that? The sunlight pouring in said it had to be mid-morning already.

But Damon was at the table, a coffee-cup in one hand, the other scrawling his initials at the bottom of each page of a lengthy document. He looked up with a smile. 'Awake already? You looked so peaceful, I didn't want to disturb you.'

The comment gave her an unpleasant little twinge; had the joy of waking her up to make love to her dissipated so quickly?

'Don't get up,' she said. But he was already on his feet, pulling a chair out for her. The one across the table, she saw, held a slim leather briefcase, open and full of papers bound in a rainbow of coloured folders. 'And it's not "already", is it? It must be late——'

'You're wondering why I'm still here at this hour. To tell the truth, I overslept.' He kissed her, long and tenderly. 'Entirely your fault, of course,' he said softly, and kissed her again before he sat down once more. 'And if you think I'm complaining, you're wrong.'

Humphrey came in with a plate full of waffles and sausage. 'Mrs Kendrick,' he said in surprise. 'I'm sorry, I didn't hear you.'

'Take that back to the kitchen, Humphrey, until Mrs Kendrick's breakfast is ready.'

Lacey shook her head. How beautiful that title sounded on his lips, she thought, and told herself not to be foolish. What else was he supposed to call her, anyway? 'No, Humphrey. I'd just like coffee, anyway. Damon, don't let your breakfast get cold.'

'Are you sure? We could share till yours is ready.' Damon cut a bite-sized bit from the corner of the waffle and held the fork out invitingly. 'Or are you hoping I'll eat and run, so you'll be rid of me?'

'No,' she said honestly. She curled her hands around her coffee-cup and thought about how pleasant it could be to share a breakfast-table every day...

'Then have a bite. You can't live on coffee, you know. Even Humphrey's coffee.' He reached for the folder that he'd been working on.

Just as easily as that, she thought, he's forgotten me.

For an endless moment, his long brown hand hovered over the folder, and then, with a half-smile, he picked it up and put it on top of the stack in the briefcase. 'I've got too used to my own company, I think,' he said. 'Working at mealtimes is a bad habit. Can I tempt you to a bite of sausage, *madame*?'

She shook her head, and he sighed and ate the savoury brown link himself. 'You're trying to waste away on me before we go to Phoenix, is that it?'

'Phoenix?' She was honestly at a loss.

'Three weeks from Friday the new hotel opens. That's what I'm doing this morning—reviewing the final details, and the reports from the new manager.'

Her heart was beginning to vibrate oddly. 'And you're going?'

He raised an eyebrow. 'Somebody has to cut the ribbon. It's a terribly tough job, but they pay me well. Shall we plan to stay a few days and play a little golf, perhaps?'

Don't be an idiot, she told herself. Making a date for three weeks ahead isn't exactly an indication that he's planning for a lifetime, you know!

Still, he had asked her to go. And it was an official corporation function. He wouldn't have taken his mistress to the opening of a new hotel, surely?

And how would you know that? she asked herself crossly. He didn't precisely say you'd be in the front row of the audience for all the world to see. You might be as safely tucked away in a discreet suite as any mistress ever was.

I don't care, she thought. He wants me a little, at least, and that's enough for right now. 'I'll have to check with my social secretary, but I don't think I've got anything planned that weekend,' she said offhandedly.

Damon grinned at her, his eyes dancing. Then he touched a finger to the sticky syrup on his plate and with lightning speed planted a dab just under each of her ears.

She jerked away and pulled her hair up into an awkward ponytail, gasping, 'Why did you do an idiotic thing like that?'

'Don't you know?' He pushed his chair back and came around the table to stand behind her. 'So I can have the pleasure of licking it off, of course. Why else?'

And, as his mouth sought out the sensitive triangle under her ear, she thought, I will stay until he tells me to go. It may be a bitter end, but surely it is better to have a handful of happiness to take with me than none at all? I will absorb all I can of caring, and that will keep me warm through the inevitable, endless days to come.

It will simply have to, she thought.

CHAPTER NINE

IN THE next couple of weeks it quickly became a pleasant routine, the two of them having a quiet breakfast together before Damon went to work. After a few days, Lacey even broke down and started to eat with him. Damon didn't say anything, but she thought he watched her with satisfaction every morning as she polished off a Spanish omelette or a pile of pancakes or a couple of Humphrey's wonderful bacon and cheese muffins.

Sometimes they talked about books; she'd been browsing the shelves of his library in an attempt to banish boredom, and he told her about the thrill of hunting down a rare early edition. Sometimes they talked about the trip to Phoenix, and what they planned to do there. Sometimes he told her about his job. But, she noted with pleasure, he didn't bring a briefcase to the table again.

'You're a bad influence, you know,' he accused one morning as they finished their coffee. 'I'm never on time to the office any more, and my desk is piled with work.'

'Yes, and I know exactly how much it bothers you,' Lacey said demurely. 'I ran into your secretary in the lobby yesterday, and she told me about the buoyant, magnanimous mood you've been in lately.'

He growled, playfully. 'Oh, you're spying on me, too, are you? It would serve you right if I didn't even go to work today.'

For an instant she almost laughed aloud with happiness. If he would put a day with her ahead of business . . .

'The entire sixteenth floor would probably chip in to send me flowers as a thank-you,' she mused.

'They would consider it a holiday if I didn't show up, that's right. And so would I.' He gave her a lazy half-smile that reminded her of what they had shared just an hour before, when he had found her in the shower. Just thinking about it made her feel ticklish all over again. He had been so very persuasive, and the rush of hot water against her skin had combined with the slick, soapy touch of his hands to create a sensual dream...

Then she remembered, and said, with a shrug, 'Sorry, but I can't spend the day with you. I've got a lunch date with Julia Patterson.'

He tossed his napkin down and came around the table to stand behind her chair. 'So break it,' he whispered. His breath was warm against her ear and his hands slid gently to cup her breasts. 'I'll take you to lunch.'

'Can't.' Her voice was steady, which was a lot more than she could say for her breathing. 'Julia and I swore when we were still in grammar school that we'd never break a date with each other for the sake of a mere man. You just didn't ask in time.'

'A mere man?' he protested. 'What kind of a mistress are you, anyway, my sweet Lacey? I demand to see your appointment book.'

Mistress. It was like a knife to her heart.

Humphrey said, from the doorway, 'Mr Kendrick, your tailor is here.'

'See?' Damon said. 'I'd forgotten all about him. You drive everything else straight out of my head, Lacey.' He went off, whistling.

It was the kind of glib, flirtatious line that he specialised in, she thought wearily. And you've been idiot enough to let yourself forget that it's no more than that.

Asking for my appointment book, indeed! And just what would he do with it? Certainly he wouldn't scrawl his name across all the pages for the entire year to come. She had almost allowed herself to forget the fact that he had said nothing about the future, beyond the trip to Phoenix, which was now less than a week away...

When she passed through the living-room a little later, she found herself in the middle of a disagreement. 'I really have better things to do today than stand still for a complete set of measurements,' Damon was saying good-naturedly. 'You know I haven't changed an inch in the last five years.'

'That was before you were a married man,' the tailor said adamantly. 'You'll find that a little contentment soon shows up in the waistline.'

Lacey wouldn't have been surprised at an explosion, but Damon only laughed. 'All right. But have a heart and make it quick, will you? I'm trying to set up a date with my wife.'

It was the first time, to her knowledge, that he had ever used the word, and it tugged at her heart like a golden chain. Then she remembered that he had only said it because the tailor was there. When they were alone, she was only his mistress...

It's not going to get easier, she told herself. With every day that goes by, it's becoming harder to remember that this isn't real. It's only a fantasy you're living in for a while, and soon all the rosy clouds will vanish...

And when he asked her opinion on the fabric samples laid out across the couch—samples from which he would select his clothes for the coming winter season—she swallowed hard and helped him choose and tried not to remember that she might never see him wearing these things at all...

'Come on,' he said, after the tailor had gathered up his belongings. 'Let's get out of here before anybody else shows up.'

'I meant it, Damon. I really can't break my lunch date.'

He looked at her for a long moment like a scolded puppy. 'What's so important about having lunch with Julia today?'

Because I can't just submerge myself in you completely, she wanted to say. It would be so easy to do, and so disastrous later, when the time comes that you don't want me any more, and there's nothing left of me except the part that loves you...

'Well, for one thing,' she said briskly, 'I'm going to ask her for a job.'

He raised an eyebrow, but he didn't question her. 'Lunch with Julia can't take all day. Come with me this morning; I promise you won't be late.'

She knew she should refuse, for her own peace of mind. If she did, he'd go to work, and that would be the end of it. It would be much more sensible not to give in. But she couldn't resist the self-confident appeal in those dark eyes, and her own heart telling her to take advantage of every minute she could have with him, so she nodded.

In the elevator, he asked, 'Why do you want a job, anyway?' He sounded curious, no more, but she felt a little defensive. 'You didn't seem to mind leaving the Clinton.'

'You didn't give me much of a chance to object. I'd rather not argue about it, Damon.'

'Who's arguing? I just want to know why you want a job.'

She sighed. 'Because I need something constructive to do with my time. I'm used to being busy, and I can't stand another single day of window-shopping. There is nothing for me to do in the apartment. I can't even beat Humphrey to the telephone when it rings, much less do anything important.'

And the excess of time on my hands, she could have added, leaves me with nothing to do but think about you, and that only encourages me to dream foolish dreams...

He shrugged. 'Julia will probably be delighted to have you. Volunteers are hard to come by.'

Lacey opened her mouth, and then shut it. She certainly wasn't going to tell him that she intended to look for a job that paid!

'Just don't let her take up all your time.' He took her hand and drew her into the small florist's shop in the Kendrick's lobby. 'I have a fancy for filling it up myself for a while.' He bought a small bunch of violets, deep-throated things in a wonderful shade of creamy white, and pinned the flowers to the lapel of her bronze-coloured jacket himself.

'Lucky girl,' Lacey heard the sales assistant say under her breath, and she thought, lucky? Well, perhaps. But for how long?

She took a deep, determined breath and put that question behind her. 'Where are we going?' she asked as they reached the street.

'Do we have to go anywhere in particular?'

His voice was husky, and it did strange things to her insides. 'You said you'd take me to your favourite bookshop,' she reminded.

He sounded surprised. 'You'd really like to go?'

She nodded, and thought, I'd move into the public library if that was what you wanted, Damon. Why would I quibble about visiting a dusty old bookshop?

'I thought perhaps you were just being polite about my strange hobbies.'

Play the game, she reminded herself. 'I'm indulging you,' she said lightly. 'See? I'm a better mistress than you give me credit for being.' She stopped and looked up at the age-darkened façade of the Clinton and wondered what the stone would look like after it was sand-blasted. Or was he planning to clean it at all?

He followed her gaze to the top of the building, and said, 'Lacey, I should run up for five minutes and just see how the workers are doing.'

She shook a playful finger at him. 'I thought you weren't going to work today. Tell the truth—you're addicted to it.'

He grinned. 'Oh, no, this is sheer joy. You can't believe the thrill of walking around in a hard hat, breathing concrete dust and listening to jackhammers. Want to come along?'

'Of course. I can't stand to miss out on so much fun. Besides, I suspect your definition of five minutes may not agree with mine.'

'All right, troublemaker. But brace yourself—it's changed.'

Her eyes widened in shock the instant they stepped out of the elevator on the top floor. The old penthouses had vanished, their walls stripped away entirely to leave great chunks of clear space. How was it possible, she thought dimly, to have done all this in just a few days?

Damon seemed to read her mind. 'This is nothing. It will take a lot longer to put it back together.'

There was neither concrete dust nor jackhammers, and the workmen who were scurrying about apparently knew exactly what they were doing. Lacey wandered around, careful of coils and piles and stacks of construction materials, while Damon and a young man in a hard hat studied a roll of blueprints.

'It looks as if a missile hit it,' she said when he rejoined her. 'I can't believe that you can make it pay, Damon. This——' She shook her head. She was half horrified at the extent of the work, and half glad that she hadn't tried to tackle the project herself.

'Don't fret. This is the worst of it, actually. On the rest of the floors we won't have to take out all the walls.'

'What was wrong with them up here?'

He smiled down at her and waved a careless hand towards the window wall. 'Look at the view—oh, sorry. I forgot that all the glass has been boarded up. Imagine the view——'

'I remember it; it's wonderful from up here. Why?'

'Is it fair to reserve that sight for the few people who can afford to rent huge suites?'

'Well, I didn't expect you to have any qualms about it,' Lacey began. 'You kept most of the top floor of the Kendrick for yourself.'

'The top floor of the Kendrick was not suitable for a restaurant. This one is. I've always thought your father missed a sure bet.'

'A restaurant,' she said thoughtfully. It made sense; the view, no matter what time of day, would be superb. And it was apparent, from the progress of the work, that he hadn't thought all of this up in the last couple of weeks, either. He'd been working on it much longer than that . . .

Don't forget, she reminded herself, that he offered to buy the place two years ago. Before he did that, he must have had some plans drawn up, no matter how tentative. And of course he hadn't thrown them away. Don't give yourself too much credit, Lacey, my girl.

He took her down the fire stairs to the floor below and showed her the way the new suites would be arranged. 'The entire hotel will be suites,' he said. 'Luxury accommodation is the thing that is really lacking in this part of town, and we underestimated the demand when we renovated the Kendrick. The smallest thing in the whole hotel will be a bedroom with a sitting-room attached. The largest will be three bedrooms and a living-room. It will allow families to travel in comfort, and it will allow business people to entertain in their suites. They'll love it.'

'First class,' she murmured.

'You did insist on that.'

'I didn't think you were really listening,' she admitted.

'And even though you think the Kendrick is beautiful, you didn't quite trust me, did you?'

'Well——'

He tapped the tip of her nose gently with his index finger. 'Let that be a lesson to you, my sweet Lacey. Now, I think you said something about a bookshop?'

The rest of the morning passed in a sort of glorious blur, spent in the remote corners of a book-lover's paradise, and when Lacey realised the time she could hardly believe it. She jumped up from the stack of books she'd been sitting on. 'I really have to go,' she said. 'Julia's going to pick me up in just a few minutes.'

Damon put the first edition he was looking at back on the shelf and reached over to brush dust off the back of her skirt with what seemed to Lacey like unnecessary care.

'Aren't you going to buy that?' she asked.

'Not if it means I can't walk back with you. Will you wait for me?'

'I guess Julia wouldn't mind if I'm a minute late,' she whispered, and when he rewarded her with a smile that was like a floodlight her heart twisted.

But Julia's car wasn't under the canopy when they got back to the Kendrick Kansas City. Damon looked around and said mildly, 'For your information, Lacey, I make it a point never to stand a lady up.'

Lacey glared at him. 'You needn't sound so self-righteous. She's just a couple of minutes late.'

'Are you certain Julia has the same interpretation of your childhood vow that you do?' he went on remorselessly, but there was a glint in his eyes. 'I'll bet if David asked her out to lunch——'

She decided to ignore him. If he wanted to stand there on the pavement and harass her, that was up to him, but she didn't have to listen! Instead, she looked over his shoulder at the window of the small jewellery shop that occupied one corner of the Kendrick's ground floor, and couldn't prevent herself from releasing a tiny gasp.

Damon turned around to look. 'Quite nice,' he said finally.

Lacey put her nose against the heavy glass to admire the necklace displayed there against a black velvet background. Tiny spotlights drew out the iridescent loveliness of a single, huge freshwater pearl in the shape of a teardrop, suspended inside an openwork gold mounting set with rows of tiny diamonds. 'It's gorgeous,' she whispered.

'Want it? I think that could be arranged.' He slipped an arm around her and added, 'You've been an exceptionally good girl lately, haven't you?'

Something snapped deep inside her. 'I didn't ask you to buy it for me,' she said furiously. 'I don't want that, or any other sort of bribe!'

His eyebrows went up. 'That was not exactly what I had in mind,' he said coolly. 'But if it would make you feel better, buy it yourself.'

With your money? she wanted to snap. Just what difference would that make? It would be every bit as much a payment for my favours!

'Not just now,' she said stiffly.

'Don't wait too long. That's a one of a kind item.' Then his eyes narrowed. 'You haven't spent your entire quarter's income already, have you, Lacey?'

The accusation was like sandpaper against her nerves. 'No,' she snapped, and then regretted it as an ominous silence descended.

A horn sounded, and she turned to see Julia's little car pull up under the canopy. Without a word to Damon, she dashed across and got in. He was still standing there, frowning, his hands on his hips, when the car slipped into traffic and turned the corner.

Several times, as they ate crabmeat quiche at Felicity's, Lacey braced herself to ask Julia if she knew of a job. She knew she should; she had been working it out in her head all week, and it was the only thing that made sense. This episode with Damon wasn't going to last forever; there were cracks around the edges already, and they weren't going to get any smaller. When it ended she would have to go back to a regular job and support herself, and getting a position would be even harder if she'd been entirely without work in the meantime.

And yet, Julia was so happy for her, so delighted that things had worked out to a story-book conclusion, that Lacey couldn't quite bring herself to cast a cloud over her friend's pleasure. If she were to say, By the way, Julia, I really need a pay cheque because I've made a vow not to spend a single penny of Damon's money—well, any variation of that was bound to cause questions, and Julia had never hesitated to ask the uncomfortable ones.

So she didn't ask, and instead they talked about old friends, and Kansas City politics, and how they really ought to join a health club and get some exercise...

Meaningless things, Lacey thought sadly, because we don't have the important ones in common any more.

'If only there were more hours in the day,' Julia lamented. 'You don't know how lucky you are, Lacey.'

And Lacey, who longed for the hours to pass faster, thought painfully, Julia is the one who is lucky. Her husband loves her, and she has a darling baby that they both adore.

She buttered a popover that she didn't want, and changed the subject, trying to forget the flash of jealousy that had twisted her heart into a knot.

The doorman at the Kendrick Kansas City touched his fingers to the brim of his hat and said, 'Mr Kendrick wanted me to ask you to come up to his office, please.'

Like a child called on the carpet, she thought. Leaving messages with the doorman! 'Thank you,' she said crisply, and went up to the apartment instead.

Humphrey looked disturbed.

'I know,' she said. 'Mr Kendrick wants to see me.'

'Yes, ma'am. He asked me to be sure you came down. I'll show you the way.'

'What if I don't want to go?'

'Perhaps it would be wise to humour him,' Humphrey said gently.

'That's the biggest problem around here,' Lacey grumbled. 'Everybody humours him.' But she reluctantly retraced her path to the lobby and took a public elevator up to the corporate floor. Even that fuelled her fury; she was certain that this wasn't the way Damon got to work.

Then she waited for what seemed forever outside the closed walnut door of his office, thumbing through a magazine, listening to the staccato clatter of his secretary's typewriter, and thinking, for a man who wasn't worried about taking the entire day off, he's certainly absorbed in something in there...

The 'something' turned out to be Bree. Her platinum-blonde hair was swept up into a smooth knot today, and the long fingernails were painted pale green to match her dress. She was carrying a briefcase—probably for camouflage, Lacey told herself irritably, as the secretary showed her into Damon's office.

It was a big room on a corner of the building, with a glorious view. But Lacey didn't see the view; she saw only Damon, rising from behind a paper-strewn desk. 'Sit down,' he said.

She ignored the request. 'Damon, was it really necessary to embarrass us both by making me come here? Getting the message from Humphrey was bad enough, but to have the doorman order me to report to your office——'

He looked at her for a long moment. 'Are you foolish enough to be upset because Bree was here, Lacey?'

'Of course not. I'm upset because I'm here!'

'Very well. Shall we get this conversation out of the way, then? About this matter of your bank account——'

'Are you certain you should be spending valuable company time discussing this?' she asked sarcastically. 'Don't you think it could have waited till this evening? It would have made wonderful dinner conversation.'

The look he gave her was a direct and uncompromising stare, and Lacey felt a little sliver of uneasiness come to life in the pit of her stomach.

But his voice was patient. 'You really meant it this morning when you said you'd had your fill of window-shopping, didn't you? Why haven't you used any of the money? I called the bank today and found out that you haven't written a single cheque on that account.'

She said stiffly, 'Don't you think it's my business whether I spend money or not?'

'Not entirely.' He tapped a pen on the blotter. 'Have you lost the cheque-book?'

'Do you think I'm likely to be so careless?' She pulled it out of her handbag and threw it on his desk.

He picked it up and tossed it back to her. She let it fall to the floor without making an effort to catch it.

His jaw tightened. 'Dammit, Lacey, that money is yours. Spend it as you like.'

'I don't want it.'

'But you have to have clothes and things—'

'What are you expecting me to buy? A constant parade of costumes like the one you so enjoyed that first night? No, thanks, Damon! I don't care what you do with that money, but I'm not going to touch it. This discussion is ended.' She turned on her heel.

'No, it's not.'

She didn't hear him. She hadn't paid any attention, when she came in, to the wall of bookshelves that flanked the doorway; it had been at her back. But now she could see it, and she stopped dead in the centre of the room. She didn't see the colourful book bindings in the case or the piece of smooth bronze sculpture in the central niche. All she saw was a gold boot on a shelf, the mate to the one on the mantel up in the penthouse, with a half a dozen yellow and white carnations nodding proudly over the top of their unusual vase.

Something seemed to tear inside her. *A trophy,* she thought. *An unusual curiosity. My mistress——*

'It's bad enough upstairs,' she said grimly. 'But must you flaunt what I am to everyone who walks into your office, as well? Tell me, what did Bree think of it?'

'Bree was here on business, Lacey, arranging hotel packages for her travel agency.'

She heard him, but she didn't care. She picked up the boot and turned it neatly and purposefully upside-down over his desk. Carnations, greenery, water cascaded over the papers scattered there. Then she dropped the boot in the middle of the mess and walked out, her spine rigid, her head high.

Her head was pounding, and there was a horrible sick feeling in her stomach. Why did you make such a scene? she asked herself frantically. Why, no matter how angry you were, didn't you just smile coldly and ignore it, and not let him see that you cared?

Because, the answer came from some unexpected corner of her brain, you weren't just angry. You were hurt because he made it so clear this morning that the way he thinks of you hasn't changed an iota. And you were scared, too—from the instant the doorman told you that Damon wanted to see you in his office. You were frightened that he was going to end it all right there, in a cold and businesslike manner, in his office, and tell you that he couldn't wait till tonight because he wanted you gone by then.

And yet, she admitted, in a way, you were hoping that he would do exactly that. No matter how painful it was, at least it would be over, and you haven't the strength to end it yourself. So, when he didn't tell you what you expected to hear, you deliberately did the most destructive thing you could think of, and tried to provoke the very thing that terrifies you most.

She didn't want to think about how important the papers on his desk might have been.

She went back to the apartment because she didn't know where else to go. Humphrey took one look at her and went off, soft-footed, to brew her a cup of tea. She was drinking it when Damon came in, more to avoid hurting Humphrey's feelings than because she wanted it.

'I'm surprised the place is still standing,' Damon said.

She didn't look up. 'I'm sorry for destroying your papers,' she said dully.

'Lacey, why?' He sat down beside her on the loveseat, cautiously, as if he half expected her to strike out at him. 'There's really no need for you to be jealous of Bree, you know.'

Her temper started to boil. 'Is that all your monumental ego can see? You really don't understand, do you?'

His fingers toyed gently with a loose lock of hair. 'I don't understand all the fuss you're making over a bit of spending money, no.'

'You're the one who made the fuss about the money,' she said stubbornly. 'It wasn't me.'

He took the cheque-book out of the inside breast pocket of his jacket. 'You're being completely irrational about this, you know. Just how long do you think you can go without cash?'

'I don't know. How long do you think this affair is going to last?'

'You're certainly doing your best to end it. You seem to think I'm paying you for your presence in my bed.'

'Aren't you?' she said sweetly. 'I'm afraid I am quite unable to make these fine distinctions, Damon.'

A tiny muscle at the corner of his mouth went taut. 'Damn it, Lacey, you enjoy making love as much as I do. And you have to have money now and then—what's the big deal about me giving it to you? I can't understand why we can't just enjoy each other for a while, without bringing all these moral judgements into it!'

That's right, she thought, you can't understand. If you had the least sensitivity, Damon Kendrick, you would never even have suggested this affair—this farce of a marriage. No one would have to explain it to you...

'Please,' she whispered, 'you've taken everything else, Damon. Let me keep my pride, at least.'

His jaw tightened. He put the cheque-book back in his pocket, and without a word he rose and went off to shut himself in his library.

Lacey buried her face in a cushion and tried to cry the pain away.

CHAPTER TEN

LACEY quickly found that all her pride did not keep her warm. All the tears she had shed did not soothe the ache in her heart. And all the longing she felt for things to be different did not open the firmly closed door of Damon's library.

When, after more than an hour, there was still no sound from him, she dragged herself up from the love-seat. She had demanded to be left with her pride; now pride said there was only one thing left for her to do. She could leave quietly, before he had to ask her to go. Before there was another scene.

She had spread her suitcases out on the big bed, and she was packing dresses, each careful fold precisely square against the satin coverlet, when she heard the door open.

It's Humphrey, she thought, even as the logical half of her brain reminded that he would never open a door without knocking. Her fingers began to tremble, and the neat folds of the sheer apricot-coloured dress seemed to dissolve between her hands.

'What the hell are you doing?' Damon's voice was low.

She didn't turn. 'What does it look like?'

'Humphrey said you were packing, but——'

'Humphrey is a damned busybody,' she said crossly. 'I wish I understood how he knows all these things! He certainly hasn't been in here——' She realised that she was babbling, and that the grip of her hands on the apricot dress was causing damage that might well be permanent. She laid it out again and folded it, with a great deal less care, and flung it into the suitcase.

'Lacey, surely you aren't going to take all of this to Phoenix? It's only a weekend trip, after all.'

'Who said I was packing for Phoenix? Was that another of Humphrey's brainstorms?' She stopped dead. He hadn't sounded cynical, or as if he was trying to pass the whole thing off as a joke. He had sounded almost sad, she thought.

'You certainly aren't going anywhere else.' The words were uncompromising, but his voice was soft, and there was a hint of uncertainty in the undertones.

She turned to face him, with a silky blouse clutched in her hands as if it was a shield. 'Damon, after the battle we had this afternoon, you surely can't expect me to stay?'

He rubbed his jaw with the back of his hand.

She whispered, 'And you can't still want me to come to Phoenix with you——'

'The hell I can't,' he said huskily. 'I do.'

Her heart started to pound, an awkward, irregular timpani rhythm.

'Think about this morning, Lacey,' he said softly. 'You can't tell me that you didn't enjoy yourself this morning.'

'Oh, you're very skilful in the shower, I'll admit that.'

His face tightened. 'That wasn't what I meant, and you know it. Or at least, that wasn't all I meant.'

She nodded, finally, unwillingly. There had been moments this morning, at the Clinton, at the bookstore, when she had been thrilled simply to be alive, and beside him.

'What the hell changed this afternoon?' he demanded harshly.

I changed, she thought. I wanted certainties. I wanted promises . . .

But there are no guarantees, she thought. No one has the assurance of happiness. Not even Julia, with her perfect family, can be certain that tomorrow it will be the same. One accident, one illness, could destroy that perfect little family overnight.

So why, she asked herself, do I insist on promises that Damon isn't capable of making? This afternoon, I would have even accepted empty promises, knowing all the while that they were empty, just for the false security they would let me feel.

Whatever it was that had made him feel marriage was a trap and lifetime commitment an impossibility, at least he was honest about his feelings. Far more honest than I am, Lacey thought. I love him. I want him. And yet I am willing to walk away from the man I love because he will not—cannot—pledge that in a year he will still want me, or in five years, or even in six months. But which of us is given that sort of guarantee?

Marriages were made every day between people who swore to love each other until death parted them. But a lot of those same people were in the divorce courts in a year...or five years...or even six months.

And if he still wants me after the kind of scene I put on in his office this afternoon, she realised, is it so hopeless to think that some day he might learn that love isn't only a word?

He saw the softness come into her eyes, and he held out his arms to her. 'Lacey, please stay,' he whispered.

Forever is such a hopeless thing to ask, she thought, when we only have today. But perhaps the truth is that, if we use it properly, we only need today...

It was, at first, a fragile peace that lay between them. They tiptoed around the subject of money, and they avoided looking at the windows of the jewellery shop whenever they went in and out of the Kendrick Kansas City.

And if sometimes the terrible nagging voice of doubt tormented Lacey, most of the time she could drown it out with the power of reason. The only guarantee we're given is that no one has forever, she would tell herself sternly. Today is what matters. Only today.

And throughout those days, it seemed, Damon was determined to keep things running smoothly, to get them back to that easy footing of the morning they had spent at the bookshop. The gold-sequinned boot quietly disappeared from the mantel, for instance, the afternoon before Lacey's parents came to dinner, and throughout the evening Damon was the perfect host and the charming companion.

Lacey had been dreading the occasion, the first time since the sham of a wedding ceremony that they had spent a number of hours alone with her parents. It seemed to her that it was going to be impossible to get through the evening without a slip of the tongue, and Bill and Ginny weren't fools...

Ginny took her aside after dinner. 'Are you all right, dear? You look a bit pale, and you ate scarcely anything.' She smoothed Lacey's hair.

'I'm fine, Mother. Well—no, I'm not, exactly. I think the high pollen count is bothering me this year. I'm just not used to it after living in New York.' She laughed a little. 'I'm sniffling and sneezing and going around with red-rimmed eyes all the time, too.' Then she held her breath. To say nothing of the stress of conversations like this, she thought. My stomach is so tied up in knots, it's a wonder I could eat anything at all tonight, but I'll feel better as soon as they go home...

'It has been dreadful, hasn't it? But now that autumn's on the way, it will be better soon.'

For an instant, Lacey didn't quite know whether to be happy that her mother had cheerfully accepted her explanation, or irritated because Ginny's famous maternal instinct had failed so badly. Don't be crazy, she told herself. Of course I'm glad she bought that story. I could run into her on Main Street tomorrow with tears flowing down my face, and she'd think twice before she accused me of crying.

'And perhaps the dry air in Phoenix will be good for you,' Ginny went on. 'Of course, George and Elinor say this isn't the best time of year to go.'

Damon said almost the same thing the next afternoon, within fifteen minutes after their plane took off from the Kansas City airport. 'It's a horrible time of year to go to Phoenix, really. But this gets the hotel up and running well before the high season starts.'

'I think it's dreadful, the sacrifices that your job requires,' Lacey told him with mock sympathy. 'I suppose they'll make you stay in a suite, too, and try out all the restaurants.'

He made a face at her. 'You'll think it's dreadful when you step into one-hundred-and-ten-degree heat, my dear. The natives get acclimatised, but for us northerners it's a different story. If you like, though, we'll come back next winter when we can bask in it.'

Next winter... 'And check on how the hotel is doing,' she said, a little breathlessly.

Damon smiled. 'Of course we'll check on the hotel. That should take us half a day or so. Or maybe we should spread it out, and study the hotel for an hour every day for a week.'

It made her feel all pleasantly soft inside. 'And the rest of the time?'

'I'm sure we can think of something to do. And if we weren't in the middle of a plane, I'd show you an example or two.'

Lacey laughed delightedly. Yes, she thought. It was going to be all right, after all. Next winter, they would come back to Phoenix... and perhaps the winter after that...

Don't get ahead of yourself, she warned. Remember that it's today that matters.

It was mid-afternoon when their plane landed, and it was indeed very hot. It was, however, a dry heat that was actually less enervating than Kansas City's climate could be, Lacey thought.

A long white Cadillac limousine met them at the airport, complete with a young assistant manager, very nervous at having the chairman of the board as his personal responsibility. He stammered that the general manager would have met them himself, except...

'I imagine he's got more important things to do,' Damon said gently.

'Yes, sir. I mean—of course not, sir! I mean——' The young man looked miserable. 'I'll help with the luggage, sir.'

'That wasn't kind,' Lacey said. She sank into the soft leather seat and looked out through the darkened window.

'He has to learn to handle awkward questions some time.'

'Do you always travel this way?' she asked.

'The limousine? No. Usually I try to slip in, incognito, by taxi, but that's getting harder and harder to do. Besides, on an occasion like this, the display is expected.'

'You could have told me.' Lacey did her best to sound peevish. 'If I'd known I was going to be a celebrity, I would have worn my dark glasses and my big picture hat to frustrate the hordes of photographers.'

Damon grinned. 'I think it would make a much better picture if we were to indulge ourselves in a bit of love-making on the way, and get out of the car a little dishevelled, but smiling.'

The young manager joined them, and the car slowly moved into traffic. 'Mr Bradford would have been here, of course,' he said, in a rush, as if he'd rehearsed the sentence for the last five minutes and was determined to say it all before he forgot it, 'but there were a great many details that needed his attention, and he feels a general manager's place is in the hotel.'

'I quite agree,' Damon murmured. 'And by the way, you should practise that firm tone of voice; it will come in handy throughout your career.'

The young man's mouth dropped open. 'You mean you're not angry that he didn't meet you?'

'I'd have been disappointed if he had. Especially on opening day, a new hotel needs a firm hand on the reins. That's why I gave Tom Bradford the job.' Damon investigated the contents of the built-in bar. 'Champagne, my dear?'

'No, thanks,' Lacey said. 'Not at this hour.'

Damon leaned back. 'All the comforts of home,' he said.

Except, Lacey could almost hear him thinking, for the intrusive presence of the nervous young manager...

There were no hordes of photographers. In fact, there was only the general manager waiting for them in the lobby. Lacey managed a very creditable disappointed-sounding sigh, and won a smile from Damon before he was absorbed in a discussion of the arrangements for the opening ceremonies.

She took advantage of the opportunity to look around. The architect had been influenced by Spanish designs, and the hotel was built around a courtyard that resembled a lush garden. The desert colours had been carried inside: restful beiges and soft golds and dusky greens that made the open spaces inviting to the eye.

This was the official grand opening day, but the hotel had been quietly receiving guests for a week, Damon had told her, making sure the new staff members had been properly trained and that everything would operate smoothly on the ceremonial day. So she wasn't surprised to see a couple of people in the pool, behind a glass wall to one side of the garden, and some at the piano bar across the lobby. Indeed, there was a sort of excited hum about the whole place.

Was this what the Clinton would feel like, when it was done? she wondered. It would look very different, of course—but would it have this feeling of newness, of wonderful things just waiting to happen?

'Would you like a tour before I show you to your suite?' the young manager asked.

'That would be——' Lacey began.

'I think we'll freshen up first,' Damon said smoothly.

In the elevator, she said mildly, 'Damon, I'd like to see the hotel.'

'My dear, you look exhausted.' His voice was solicitous. 'You'll enjoy it much more after you've had a nap.'

The young manager unlocked the suite door and handed over the keys. 'If there is anything else——'

'We'll call,' Damon promise. He ushered the young man out and locked the door, then tossed the keys on to the table in the sitting-room, between an arrangement of fresh flowers and a basket of fruit, and reached for Lacey.

'I'm not tired, Damon.'

He grinned. 'I was hoping you'd say that,' he murmured wickedly, and kissed her in a way that left no doubt about his plans. 'I've been wanting to do that since we boarded that damned plane,' he said softly. 'Every time you looked at me, or smiled—— It's inhuman to treat a man that way, my sweet Lacey, when he can't do anything about it.'

'You have a hotel to open in two hours, Damon.'

'Good. That gives me an hour to make love to you.' He picked her up and pushed the bedroom door open with his shoulder to carry her in. 'And I'm going to enjoy every minute of it.'

'The bellboy will be coming up with our bags,' she said breathlessly.

'Have you noticed the luggage racks? It's a new twist my architect thought up.'

And on the racks, Lacey noted, their suitcases were already neatly in place. 'How did they do that?' she asked, her surprise driving everything else out of her head for the moment.

'Our motto is service—swift, luxurious, and discreet. Starting with the chairman of the board—or don't you want me to make love to you?'

He let her slide to the floor, as if he was going to let her go, but he made sure that her body stayed pressed firmly against his. The delightful friction sent shudders of anticipation through her, and she whispered, 'It would be a shame to waste a whole hour.' Her voice quavered a little. 'Perhaps we could postpone the tour...'

He kissed her again, his tongue probing hungrily, as if he were starving for the taste of her. Lacey made a little sound, deep in her throat, and he pulled her even closer and began to remind her of everything he had learned about her body in a month of patient research.

And a little later, he said unsteadily, 'On the way back to the airport, I think we'll have the limousine, and dispense with the assistant manager. And have the driver take the long way round...'

She was still a little dazed by the storm he had unleashed. Too relaxed to move, they lay tangled together for a long time, and when he finally, reluctantly, pulled away, she opened her eyes and murmured a protest.

'Come on,' he said. 'Remember? There's a grand opening about to start downstairs.'

'Just now, I'd like that nap you said I should have.' She yawned. 'You don't need me, do you?'

He smacked her gently. 'Of course I need you.'

She glowed just a little deep inside.

'We're taking the Bradfords to dinner after the ceremonies.'

The momentary high dissipated. 'I'll be ready in time for dinner,' she promised. 'It's just that——'

He dragged her out of the bed. 'Into the shower,' he ordered. 'When you're in this mood, I don't trust you for a minute. You'd go off to sleep and not wake up till tomorrow morning, or else you'd manage to entice me back into bed, and then we'd both be in the soup.'

'Slave-driver,' she muttered. But a happy little voice at the back of her brain whispered, he wants me, he wants me...

Still, when the general manager gave Damon a huge pair of streamer-decked scissors to cut the gold ribbon that ran the width of the lobby, she was startled when Damon turned and handed them to her. She shot a look up at him and then cut the ribbon as if she had rehearsed it for days—a lucky cut, because she almost couldn't see what she was doing for the tears in her eyes. It was such a small thing, really, and yet such a large one at the same time—a symbol to everyone who watched that he was inviting her to be a part of his real world, too, as well as his private one...

She enjoyed dinner, too, and dessert afterwards at the Bradfords' small house on the outskirts of Phoenix, feeling for the first time as if she really belonged there beside him. There was a lovely feeling of permanence about the things that had happened today...

Watch out, she reminded herself. Remember, Lacey, that forever is built of days lived one at a time—and you must not let yourself count on tomorrow, or you'll forget to enjoy today.

When the Bradfords' small son woke up, she begged the privilege of giving him his bottle, and sat quietly in a corner of the living-room, rocking the sweetest little bundle she had ever held.

She intercepted a jaundiced look or two from Damon, and she wanted to stick out her tongue at him. What was wrong with her borrowing a baby, for heaven's sake?

When she carried the sleepy infant back into his nursery, Jill Bradford said, with a smile, as she tucked the child in, 'A man on his honeymoon is always such a fun creature to watch. If his wife pays attention to anything except him, he's absolutely green. He's not much on babies at the moment, I take it?'

That was one of the world's record understatements, Lacey thought. 'Not only at the moment. Forever, I think.'

'Oh, he'll feel differently when it's his own,' Mrs Bradford said wisely. 'They all do.'

But then, Lacey thought, Damon wasn't by any stretch of the imagination the usual man...

They were in the cab for the trip back to the hotel when he said, 'I hope you're not going to make a habit of that.'

'Of playing with babies?' Her stubbornness flared; he was not going to tell her what to do with every moment of her time! She said firmly, 'As a matter of fact, I was thinking of offering to keep Julia's little girl now and then. I'm sure she needs a stand-by babysitter, and as long as I don't have anything else to do——'

'Lacey, don't get any crazy ideas.'

'All I did was give a hungry baby his bottle! What's crazy about that?'

His jaw tightened. 'Just don't start thinking that having a baby of your own would be a good idea. Because it wouldn't hold us together any more than that stupid piece of paper will.'

'And why would I think anything like that? I'm not deaf, and you've certainly made yourself plain enough.'

'Good.' He sighed, as if relieved. 'And as far as you having nothing to do—I was going to wait to tell you this till we got home, but perhaps this is as good a time as any.'

'Oh?' There was a wary note in her voice.

'I've arranged a job for you in the public relations department. You can start next week.'

She was stunned for an instant. The cab pulled up to the hotel, and Damon paid the fare. Lacey bit her tongue till they were inside their suite, and then she said, sharply, 'Well, isn't that charming of you? I'm sure your department head was thrilled to be told that he desperately needed another person on staff.'

'He can certainly use you, but in any case, you wanted a job, and I've found you one.'

'Don't you mean, you manufactured one?' Lacey said sweetly. 'I thought you had a little more sense that that, Damon.'

'What difference does it make if I asked him to make a place for you? You're supposed to be a public relations person worth your salt!'

'I'm a damned good public relations person! What does this job consist of, anyway?'

'Oh, I'm not sure what he has in mind. Giving some tours, perhaps, and——'

'What a delightful position! I already feel myself in need of a substantial raise. Oh, Damon, you idiot! Don't you think I'm smart enough to know that this is just another way to give me money, to keep me depending on you? And that is exactly what I won't do, damn it. I will not take your money. Not unless——' She stopped dead.

'Unless what?'

There was a long silence. All the talk of living for today didn't sink in very far, did it, Lacey? she asked herself. You can tell yourself a million times a day, but you obviously can't make yourself believe it...

She said, lifelessly, 'Unless you're willing to say that there's a future for us.'

He threw himself into a chair. 'Lacey, for heaven's sake——'

'I mean it, Damon. Without that, I'm only your mistress, and that by itself is enough to tear me up. But if I take your money, too, then I'm no better than any prostitute walking the streets!'

'Lacey, that's completely ridiculous.' She didn't answer, and after a long time he sighed and said, 'So we're right back where we were two years ago, aren't we? You've set your terms, and I can't meet them.'

The pain was the same as if he had stabbed her. Had she been so wrong, then, in thinking that he did care about her, at least a little? Had his gesture this evening at the grand opening been just for show, after all, with no meaning at all? It's my job, now, she realised bitterly. Giving tours and cutting ribbons all fall into the same category of uselessness.

'Why?' she pleaded. 'Damon, just tell me why! If I only understood——'

He turned away. 'Would you like some cognac?'

She stared at his back for a long moment. 'No, thank you,' she said stiffly. 'I think I'll go to bed, Damon. I'm not feeling well.' From the bedroom door, she added, in a voice heavy with irony, 'I think perhaps the shellfish I had for dinner wasn't quite fresh.'

He didn't answer. She went into the bedroom, pulling pins out of her upswept hair with furious fingers, almost welcoming the pain it caused. What else was there to say? That she loved him? When he had ignored everything else she had said, he certainly wasn't going to be swayed by a proclamation of undying love!

The bed had been neatly made up again and the blankets turned back invitingly. The lamps were turned on, casting a welcoming glow across the plump white pillows. Pillows, she thought, that bore no evidence of their earlier use——

'So much for his promise to be discreet,' she muttered under her breath. She tried to tell herself that it didn't matter if the chambermaid knew that they hadn't been napping here this afternoon. On an ordinary day, it wouldn't matter a bit; it certainly wouldn't bother Damon. But tonight...

Her stomach really did hurt. But she didn't think it was the shellfish.

She woke in the small hours of the morning, as suddenly wide awake as if she had been drenched with iced water, with an abrupt certainty piercing her mind with horrifying force.

Beside her, a careful distance away, Damon lay; his breathing was even and precise.

I'm not deaf, she had told him earlier in the evening. I certainly know you don't intend to let a woman own you, or let her bear your child... You made that perfectly clear.

A child wouldn't hold us together, he had said, and she knew that; the possibility that it might had never occurred to her.

She slid carefully out of bed and pulled on a long robe, and went out on to the balcony that opened off the living-room. It was still hot, and the desert breeze teased at a wisp of her hair, dragging it across her face.

'No, I'm not deaf,' she whispered to herself. 'But possibly I have been very, very stupid...'

He had clearly said, on more than one occasion, that there never would be a child of his in this world. He had said it as if there was no doubt in his mind, and no reason for further discussion. She hadn't really questioned why he was so certain; everything had happened so fast. But she hadn't taken the precaution of going on the Pill. It had never occurred to her that it might be wise.

And yet tonight he had warned her not to think that bearing his child would be the answer to her wish for permanence. That certainly implied that such a thing was possible, after all.

She put her forehead down against the cool wrought-iron railing of the balcony.

It wasn't the shellfish that made me sick tonight, she thought. And it wasn't the stress of having my parents come to dinner that caused my indigestion last night, either.

It's the baby I'm carrying...

CHAPTER ELEVEN

WHAT a fool you are, Lacey told herself coldly, not to have seen this before, not to have suspected what was happening to you.

For this sudden insight explained everything—even the emotional roller-coaster she had been on for the last week. Now, it was so much easier to understand the way she had behaved the afternoon she had seen the boot full of flowers in Damon's office. She had been angry and scared, all right, but it was no wonder she'd handled it so badly. She had been emotionally distraught because her body had been already trying to adjust itself to pregnancy.

And what an absolute idiot she was, not to have made certain that, whatever might happen to her, she didn't bring an innocent child into this mess—a baby whose father not only didn't want him, but who might even deny his parentage altogether...

Why didn't I insist that the jerk make himself clear? she thought. Why didn't I take care of myself, no matter what he said?

Because, she thought wearily, I suppose in a way I actually wanted this to happen.

What was it Mrs Bradford had said tonight? A man feels differently when it's his own child, something like that. Had she counted on that, unconsciously?

When he offered you this travesty of marriage, she told herself, you believed deep down that you could change him—that some day he would come to love you as you love him, and that ultimately it would be all right—the two of you in a house in Sunset Hills, with a couple of kids, a station wagon, and a big, shaggy dog...

What a perfect dunce you are, she thought drearily.

But there was no profit now in figuring out why it had happened. She considered, fleetingly, the possibility that she might be mistaken, and dismissed it. The evidence was compelling; there was no doubt in her mind that she was carrying Damon's child. And she had some decisions to make.

All my life, she thought, I've taken the easy way out of things. Two years ago, when Damon didn't meet my expectations, I went to New York, where I didn't have to face him. When renovating the Clinton looked like too big a job, I backed away from it as well. I even chose a career that emphasises not substance, but skill at putting a good face on things. And now I'm stuck; I can't run away from this.

But she could. There was an easy way out of this problem too, she realised. Surely no one would blame her if she simply ended this pregnancy? If she did it soon, no one would even have to know what she had done.

But I would know, she told herself. And I could never rid myself of the knowledge that I ended my baby's life for my own convenience.

In any case, what would that accomplish? I could go on living with Damon, then, for another month, or a year. But the truth is, it's over now. I love him; I will always love him. But I can't go on any longer like this, never knowing from morning to night. And he made it plain tonight that he cannot give me any more than that. The uncertainty will weigh me down, and make both of us miserable. Better to end it now, than let it drag on into tears and recriminations and enmity, later on.

Whatever had made him what he was, it had left horrible wounds on him. She loved him in spite of it—

perhaps a bit because of it; sometimes he seemed to be a lost little boy, wearing a mask, and she wanted to know what lay behind it. But she could not force him to drop that mask. And she could not wait forever in the hope that he would heal enough to reach out to her. If the decision lay between her child and its father, there was only one choice she could make.

She had no idea how long Damon stood in the balcony door, watching her. But the darkness in the eastern sky was changing slowly to grey when he came to stand beside her at the rail, the soft breeze ruffling his hair. He didn't touch her. 'Lacey, it's getting cold out here. Come back in.'

She didn't look at him. 'I won't jump,' she said. 'I haven't the courage.'

He said something under his breath that might have been an oath.

She looked at him then—or perhaps she looked beyond him, with eyes that weren't seeing anything very clearly just then, except the decision she had made. 'Damon, I want to go home,' she said quietly, and it was more un-yielding than any amount of hysteria could have been.

'All right,' he said. 'We'll go home today.'

They didn't talk about it. They didn't talk at all.

Sometimes he looked at her as if he wanted to tell her what he was thinking, and she would hold her breath and hope—and then he would walk away.

How could I have let myself believe that we could work out our differences and be happy, she asked herself, when we can't even talk to each other?

And, though they shared the big bed in his penthouse apartment for two more nights, it was like a battlefield where a temporary cease-fire had been declared; neither of them ventured into the no man's land which separated them as effectively as any barbed-wire fence could have done.

On Monday morning, as soon as he had gone to work, she locked herself into the bathroom and confirmed her pregnancy with a home-testing kit. She had bought it at a little pharmacy in a far-away suburb on Saturday afternoon, and sneaked it into the apartment inside a Tyler-Royale shopping bag, feeling as if she was smuggling drugs and the police were likely to swarm down upon her from ambush at any minute.

Not that she really needed the chemical confirmation; her physical reaction to the sight of Damon eating scrambled eggs and bacon that morning had left little doubt that her case of indigestion wasn't going to go away soon.

And there had never really been any doubt in her mind. It was almost as if, once she had considered the possibility of pregnancy, the child had become a physical presence, as real as if there was a warm and blanket-wrapped bundle already in her arms. But it seemed only sensible to use the test to be certain that it wasn't just some horrible joke that her over-stressed body was playing on her. So she had waited, hiding her physical symptoms, until she was truly alone.

Her things took surprisingly little room. One suitcase and her overnight tote-bag; nothing that she couldn't handle by herself. That was fortunate, she thought, for she would not—could not—call the front desk and ask for a bellboy's help. It wouldn't take long for the Kendrick's grapevine to pass along that juicy bit of news, and, even though she couldn't exactly imagine Damon rushing down from his office to plead with her not to go, still, she'd just as soon slip out unnoticed.

As a matter of fact, she told herself cynically, a scene in the lobby would be no worse, as far as she was concerned, than no scene at all, which was probably what would actually happen. He might just breathe a quiet sigh of relief, instead—and, if he did, Lacey would just as soon not know.

She waited until Humphrey went out to do his daily marketing, and then she tucked her hair up under a straw hat, settled her dark glasses firmly on the bridge of her nose, propped a sealed envelope on the table in the library and arranged her rings—the shimmering diamond starburst, and the carved wedding band—beside it. Then she quietly slipped out of the Kendrick Kansas City for the last time. She could see quite clearly this time; tears did not threaten to blind her, and she had no trouble avoiding the edge of the revolving door in the lobby.

She parked her little red car behind the house in Hyde Park and crossed the patio—where it had all started, on that hot Sunday afternoon—to tap on the back door. She heard voices in the kitchen. Elinor Tanner was there, she realised. Well, everyone would know the facts soon enough anyway, and George and Elinor had been like family for as long as she could remember.

Ginny came to the door. 'Good heavens, Lacey, you're knocking? Don't you dare act like a guest in this house, or I'll turn you over my knee——' She stopped, and her eyes narrowed. 'Come in, darling.' It was gentle. 'I'll get you a cup of coffee.'

Until that moment Lacey had done it all tearlessly and calmly, with step-by-step logic. But Ginny's words—so everyday, so hauntingly normal—broke the dam. She sat at the kitchen-table holding her cup between her hands and trembling so violently that hot coffee slopped over her fingers.

'Is Dad at work?' she asked.

'No. He's playing tennis with George over at the Rockhill Club. Shall I call him?'

Lacey shook her head. 'No, I——' She swallowed hard. 'I just came to tell you that I've left Damon. I'm not going back.'

She didn't go into the details; she hoped it would never be necessary for Bill and Ginny to know the whole truth about how her marriage had come about. And she didn't say anything about the baby. There would be plenty of time for that. Flatly, she recited the bald statement that things weren't working out and there was no prospect of them working out, and so she had left.

Ginny's eyes were huge pools of sadness, but her voice was firm. 'You'll come home, of course, Lacey.'

'No. That would only make it harder on you and Dad. I don't want you to be caught in the middle. In fact, it would probably be better if you said you hadn't even seen me—if Damon calls. He probably won't. I left a note saying that I'd be in touch when I decided what to do.'

She didn't even notice when Elinor slipped away, but a few minutes later her father's arms were around her, and that was the final straw. And, while she cried out her pain into Bill Clinton's broad shoulder, the four of them—the Clintons and the Tanners—made plans. She could not just wander off without a destination, they said firmly. If she insisted on leaving Kansas City, then there was a logical place to go.

George handed her a key-ring. 'The condo's just sitting there, empty,' he said. 'We'll call our housekeeper, and she'll have the place stocked and ready for you. Stay as long as you like.'

'Arizona?' Lacey wailed. 'I can't go back to Arizona.' George and Elinor's condo in Scottsdale was perhaps half an hour away from the new hotel in Phoenix that had held both the happiest and the most hellish moments of her brief marriage. Of course, she thought, it did have one advantage; if Damon actually looked for her, he certainly wouldn't start there. So she nodded, finally, and took the keys.

She would want her car, of course, they decided. But since it was a three-day drive, they decreed that she could not go alone. Ginny could pack in fifteen minutes...

'I'm not going to do anything crazy,' Lacey said. 'I love you, Mother, but I need to be alone.'

'And you will be,' Ginny said. 'I won't question you, I won't ask for explanations. But please, Lacey, let me come along. You're my daughter, and I have to do what I can to protect my child.'

And how can I argue with that, Lacey thought, when everything I'm doing is to protect mine?

Ginny was true to her word. Before they even got to the Arizona border, she had diagnosed the main problem, Lacey was sure. But it wasn't until a week later, when Lacey took her to the airport for her flight home, that Ginny breathed a word. She hugged Lacey and said, 'I don't know if I should tell you I'm happy about the baby, which I am, or sad, because I'm that, too. But your father and I are behind you, no matter what you decide to do.'

Lacey forced herself to smile. 'Take care of yourself, Grandma,' she whispered, and knew that she had made the right choice when she saw the misty gladness dawn in Ginny's eyes.

She made a side trip on her way back to the condo, and drove by the bustling new hotel. Some day, she thought, I'll bring my son or daughter here...

On impulse, she parked the car across the street and went in. All she wanted was one of the hotel's promotional leaflets, for the baby's scrapbook, and surely, if she kept her dark glasses on, and didn't dawdle in the lobby...

Still, she heaved a great sigh of relief when she was safely back in the car. That wasn't very bright, she chided herself. What if someone had seen you, and stopped you to chat? What would you have said?

Intrigue and espionage are not my field, she thought. It's a good thing I didn't want to grow up to be a spy— I can't stand the strain!

And now there was only one more important thing to do, she told herself. Now that she had made up her mind about a few things, she would have to write to Damon.

The words did not come easily, and three days later she was still struggling. She had torn up and discarded most of a box of expensive stationery and had taken to drafting sentences on the backs of envelopes, working each word out till it seemed right.

The effort was giving her a headache. She shoved the stationery box under the edge of the couch and stuck her head into the kitchen to tell Elinor's housekeeper that she was going for a walk.

Rosa shook her head. 'Crazy,' she said succinctly.

'I'm only following doctor's orders, Rosa. She said I should take vitamins, drink milk, and go for a walk at least twice a day.'

'The doctor didn't say to walk in the heat of the afternoon,' Rosa said stubbornly.

Lacey let herself out of the condo with relief. Only now do I truly appreciate Humphrey, she thought. Rosa isn't only a housekeeper, she's more like a mother hen...

She put her shoulders back and took a deep breath and started off. It was hot, but she was dressed for it in her brief shorts and oversized T-shirt. And she wasn't going very far—just down to the little service station three blocks away. She was having a terrible craving for red liquorice...

At the kerb, a car door opened and a tall, dark-haired man stepped out. He called her name, and Lacey stopped breathing. No, she thought. There is simply no way he could know where I am.

Damon came up the walk, his stride unhurried, and stopped a precise three feet from her. 'Lacey,' he said again. There was something odd about his voice, she thought, a combination of stress and relief...

'How did you find me?' She fixed her eyes on the monogrammed breast pocket of his shirt.

'Luck. Pure luck. May I come in?'

'I was just going for a walk.'

'Then I'll come along.' He waited a moment, and said gently, 'Lacey, I need to talk to you.'

'Why now? You haven't had much to say before.'

'That's true,' he admitted.

'I left you a note.'

'Which didn't tell me anything.'

'I was going to write to you——'

'I know. Your mother told me.'

'My mother? You're not going to make me believe that my mother told you where I am!'

He didn't answer. His dark eyes were intent on her face, and he had planted himself firmly on the pavement and showed no signs of leaving. 'I need to talk to you,' he repeated.

We might as well get it over with, she thought. It shouldn't take long to convince him that I don't plan to come back. Reluctantly, she said, 'I suppose we can go sit on the patio. It's shaded there.' She took him around to the back of the condo. She sat on the edge of a chair. He took the redwood bench beside the picnic-table.

'So talk,' she said.

There was a long uneasy silence, as if he didn't know where to start. 'I don't blame you for walking out.' He was drawing patterns on the table with a fingernail, and he didn't look at her. 'I haven't given you an easy time of it for the last month.'

She didn't answer.

His dark eyes lifted to meet hers. 'You told me that if you only understood why I wouldn't promise you the future, that it might make a difference.'

She sat very still.

He sighed. 'Lacey, when I was eleven years old, and Dirk was ten, our father found our mother in one of the Kendrick's suites with her lover. My father forgave her, of course—anyone could make a mistake once, he thought, but of course it wouldn't happen again. She was a beautiful woman, and he worshipped her—we all worshipped her. And he wanted to keep the family together for Dirk's sake and mine.'

There was a long and painful silence. She ventured, finally, 'I don't quite see——'

He went on as if she hadn't said anything. 'As a matter of fact, that man wasn't the first lover she had, and he certainly wasn't the last. After that, on an average of twice a year, my father caught her with her latest—friend. I suppose "caught" isn't a very good word for it; she wasn't trying to hide. I figured out that as the years went on she took pleasure in bringing it out in the open. She—it was almost as if she was addicted to men, and as she grew older, she had to prove to herself that she could attract a man, hold him till she got tired of him, flaunt him in front of her husband—use his own hotels to make a fool of him——'

Lacey was too horrified to move.

'It went on for years, and the men kept getting younger and younger. Every time, she would charm my father back into loving her—oh, yes, she could be charming. She'd tell him she really loved only him, and that she just didn't know why she did these things. And because he adored her, he would believe her story, and accept her word that it wouldn't happen again, and take her back—and within a month it would be another man.'

Lacey's hands were clenched on the arms of her chair.

'Dirk and I were caught in the middle. We loved her, too, you see. I grew to hate that charm of hers, but even so, sometimes I was still blinded by it.'

He raised his head, but Lacey thought he probably didn't see her at all.

'And then one night when I was twenty-three, and the man in her life was a freshman in college, I walked into the living-room just as my father was pleading with her to give this boy up and to settle down. She'd been drinking, and apparently she was tired of the game. So she told him the truth that time, instead of charming him back into submission. She told him that she had never cared a molecule for him, that she had only allowed him into her bed because having his children meant she would always have a hold on him, and once she had done her duty and produced his two brats she figured he owed her the freedom to do whatever she wanted for the rest of her life.'

'Oh, dear lord,' Lacey whispered.

Damon didn't seem to hear. 'My father just stared at her for a long time, as if he'd finally seen what she really was. He didn't say a word. Then he walked away, and she laughed—she laughed! Not even Dirk knows that.'

She wanted to reach out to him, to comfort him. But she knew he was alone just now in a very private hell, and that to try to touch him would only make it worse.

'I've never hit a woman before or since, but that night——' He took a deep breath. 'I slapped her across her beautiful face. She stopped laughing, at least, and then we heard the shot...'

Lacey could almost hear it herself, echoing across the canyons of time. She whispered, 'I knew it had been a gun accident——'

Damon shook his head. 'There was nothing accidental about it, and I don't consider it suicide, either.

Oh, he pulled the trigger, all right, but she drove him to it. It was murder, pure and simple. She wore black and sobbed at his funeral, and then she retreated to the Riviera with her young friend. I haven't seen her since.'

He looked up, and his eyes were dark pools of pain. 'I swore the night my father died that I would never be caught in the trap he was. I would never give anyone that sort of power over me.'

I will never let a woman own me; there will never be a child who calls me Father... Women were dangerous; children could be used as weapons... Of course, she thought. It all made sense, in light of his emotionally battered childhood, culminating in that horrible night.

'You should have told me, Damon.'

Anger snapped in his eyes. 'What kind of fool do you think I am? Telling you would have been like giving you the recipe for how to hurt me most——'

It was like a whip laid across her tender skin. She winced under the blow. And yet, he had said she had the power to hurt him... 'So why have you told me now?' she asked quietly.

'Because, heaven help me, I've come down here to beg, to plead, to crawl, to offer you anything you want, if you'll just come back with me, Lacey. I need you—I love you.' It was a hoarse admission.

There was a lump in her throat so big that it was hard to breathe.

'I was so foolish that I didn't even recognise what was happening to me,' he went on. 'That night at your surprise party, when I saw Grant kissing you, I just knew that I didn't want him to touch you again. I married you so that you would be in my control for as long as I wanted you. I didn't want to wonder about what you were doing when you weren't with me. And all the time I was telling myself that it was really only an affair, that

I'd soon get tired of you, or if you so much as looked at another man I could throw you out and laugh——'

'Do you really think I'm like that, Damon?'

'For a long time, I've thought all women were like that,' he said simply.

'Not me.'

There was a tiny silence. 'It doesn't matter,' he said. 'Come back with me, Lacey. It will be different this time. Just the two of us.'

There was a tiny, feeble fluttering deep in the pit of her stomach. It couldn't be the baby; it was far too early for that—but it was a painful reminder, nevertheless. It was too early for the baby, she thought, and too late for the marriage. Because it would have to be the three of us... And because, even though he said he loves me, he still cannot bring himself to trust that I could not hurt him as his mother did. If it was only me, she thought, perhaps I could try again. But the baby changes so many things...

'Your mother seemed to believe that, when you'd had a chance to think it over, you might come back, Lacey.'

She shook her head. It was the hardest thing she had ever done, to hold the shimmering illusion of happiness like a soap bubble on her finger, and then to let it fall.

His shoulders slumped for a moment. Then, with dignity, he stood up. 'I have something for you in the car,' he said quietly. 'Will you wait while I get it?'

She nodded, without curiosity, and didn't even watch as he walked away. She felt, at the moment, as if she would never be able to get up again, much less walk the few feet into the house. She propped her elbows on the chair arms and put her forehead down into the palms of her hands. The heat was awful, and she was feeling just a little ill. Perhaps, she thought, I'll just sit here and die...

Rosa came out on to the back step to shake her dust-cloth. 'Well, I thought he'd never have the sense to leave,' she said. 'Now, you get yourself back into this house where it's cool, Miss Lacey, or I'm going to call up your mama and tell her you're doing your best to give that baby heatstroke——'

'Oh, put a plug in it, Rosa,' she said rudely. She jumped up from her chair.

At the same instant, Damon said, in a choked moan, 'Baby?'

And, for Lacey, everything went sort of a sickly pinkish-orange, and suddenly she couldn't stand up any more...

She never actually lost consciousness; she struggled against being carried inside, and as soon as Rosa bustled out of the room Lacey pushed herself up to sit on the edge of the couch. She couldn't quite force her muscles to co-operate in standing up, though.

'Baby?' Damon repeated.

'I don't know why you should be surprised—unless it's never quite dawned on you what causes them!' she said crossly.

'I sort of assumed that you'd do anything you could to protect yourself, Lacey.'

'And I thought when you said there would never be a child of yours, that you'd—had mumps or something!'

He smiled, a little. 'We're both pretty fair at assuming things, aren't we?'

'In any case, it doesn't matter.' She lay back against the cushions and let Rosa put a damp cloth across her forehead. 'It's too late now.'

'It's not too late for an abortion.' It was quiet.

She shot upright again. The cold cloth fell unnoticed on to the couch. 'You bastard!' she hissed. 'Do you seriously think I'm going to murder this baby, just so I can be invited back into your bed? It's not his fault that both his parents are idiots! Why don't you just go away, Damon? Go away and forget that you ever heard any of this! Or, if you can't forget, maybe you'll be able to convince yourself that this isn't your baby at all—that I must have had a lover along the way because you're so damned sure that *all women do*!'

He smiled at her, and picked up the cold cloth, and when she paused to take a breath he stuffed the corner of it into her mouth. She glared at him and spat it out.

'Is that why you ran, Lacey?' he asked quietly. 'The baby?'

'I knew you'd think I did it on purpose.' She sighed. 'And that was before I even knew about your mother. I couldn't have messed up worse if I'd tried, could I?'

'My mother would have stayed,' he said meditatively. 'You didn't leave because you just couldn't stand any more, did you?'

She leaned back and stared at the ceiling. 'Do you mean, would I have left at all if it hadn't been for the baby? Probably. I love you, Damon. It was tearing me up not to know whether you cared about me. That was all I wanted—just to know.'

'Oh, what a fool I've been,' he whispered. His fingers sought the softness of her temple, and stroked the damp hair back. 'Fighting the very thing I wanted the most— terrified that if I let myself love you, I'd be caught on the same carousel that killed my father. And all the time, every minute of the day, you were creeping a little further into my heart. Every time I said your name, it was like a secret little delight curling through me.'

'You did a good job of fighting it off.'

He smiled, a little sadly. 'I'm afraid I did, Lacey. I didn't want to think about what was happening. I just wanted things to stay as they were—it suited me just fine that way!—and when you kept forcing me to look at it from your point of view I was furious, and too scared to ask myself why it bothered me so much. And then I came home and you weren't there, just that stiff little note, and I had to face up to what I'd done.'

'I still want to know how you found me,' she whispered.

'Tom Bradford saw you in the hotel lobby. Actually, he thought he saw someone who looked a great deal like you, and it wasn't until the grapevine version reached him—and quite a story it is, too—that he realised it might really have been you. So he called me.'

'But——'

'But darned near a million people live here, so how did I manage to walk up to your door?' His smile was a little crooked. 'That was the other bit of luck. I'd been listening, you see, to your father talk about all the fun he and his friend George Tanner were going to have this winter in Scottsdale. So the instant I got off the plane I checked the telephone book and crossed my fingers while I drove out here, praying that Tom hadn't been mistaken——'

'Then it wasn't my mother, after all,' she said softly.

He shook his head. 'She didn't sound very happy about it, but she wouldn't tell me anything except that you were safe, and that you needed some time. Lacey, I really thought I was going insane, then—when she wouldn't tell me where you were. These last ten days without you have been horrible—facing up to what I'd done to you, admitting how much I love you, recognising that you might never turn up, and that I had driven away the person I want the most in the world because I was afraid——'

There was a harsh tremor in his voice that was more convincing than any number of loving words could be.

He reached into his pocket and handed her a small box—the package he had gone back to his car to get.

'This isn't a bribe,' he said. 'It isn't payment. I want you to have it because it belongs to you—with my love.'

It was the single teardrop pearl, shimmering in its gold and diamond setting. She let her hand close gently around the pendant. It was different now, she thought, accepting it with his love.

She pulled him down to her, and the necklace dropped unheeded to the carpet. His kiss was tender, soft, gentle, and altogether the most sensual caress she had ever received.

'I didn't know until you left how empty a place can be after it's had you in it,' he confessed unsteadily. 'And I didn't know what a sentimental idiot I was capable of being until all I had left of you was a pair of boots and a single gold finger-nail——'

'So you did have that fingernail,' she mused.

'I've carried it in my wallet since that morning.'

She thought about it, and smiled. I can even forgive him the boot in his office now, she thought, because now I know it wasn't just a trophy...

'That damned apartment is a tomb without you. Come back with me, Lacey?'

She wanted to agree. She wanted so much to nod, and then lose herself in the wonder of letting him show her that he loved her. But it wasn't just the two of them, any more, that had to be considered. They hadn't talked about the baby, except for that suggestion of his...

'Damon, I swear I didn't plan this. But I can't destroy the baby——'

'I know you can't, my love. I know—now.' His hand wandered across her stomach, and she caught her breath. There was no physical evidence yet, not even the slightest swelling beneath the flat muscles, and yet there was a sensation about the way he touched her that she had never imagined.

'The baby is not a pleasant shock,' he admitted honestly. 'But then it wasn't in your plans, either, was it? We created this life together; it's up to us to take care of it.'

'Him,' she said, through tears that misted her eyes. And she thought, no matter what lies ahead of us, we can handle it now. Armed with love and honesty, we can take on the world...

The work on the Clinton took nearly a year and a half, and they re-opened it just before the Christmas season with the biggest party downtown Kansas City had ever seen. Actually, the ribbon ceremonies were held twice. The first time—the unofficial one—occurred unexpectedly when Michael Clinton Kendrick, eight months old and congenitally curious, pulled himself up in his stroller to investigate the silver, red, and green ribbons that shimmered so invitingly across the width of the lobby, and succeeded in bringing the whole mess down on his curly dark head. Damon rescued his screaming son from the wreckage and said philosophically, 'I guess, if it comes to that, he's got the best qualifications of any of us to officiate at this party.' He stroked the baby's dark hair and whispered soothing nothings into his ear, and was rewarded with a watery smile.

'Except that he'd want to use his teeth instead of scissors,' Lacey said. So that night, after Michael was safely asleep in his crib with Humphrey standing guard, she cut the ribbons herself, and shed a couple of happy tears when her parents gave her a hug...

The party went on till all hours, a combination of grand opening and the wedding reception they had never had. That was why, when Lacey roused herself from a sound sleep a mere three hours after the party ended, and found Damon gone and his pillow cold, she was startled.

She found him in the nursery, sitting quietly in the rocking chair. In the crib, the baby lay on his stomach, his fist curled next to his rosy cheek, his knees drawn up under him as if sleep had caught up with him as he crawled.

'I didn't hear Michael cry,' she said, with a yawn.

'He didn't.' Damon looked a little sheepish. 'I just came in to watch him sleep for a while.'

'Oh,' she said softly, and sank down on the floor at his feet, her cheek against his knee. 'You're not just a little bit attached to him, are you?'

Damon's eyebrows arched. 'Of course not.'

'Right. Some day I'm going to tell him about you bursting into tears at the instant he was born——'

'It was one of the better moments of my life,' he admitted. His hand came to rest quietly on her hair. 'Lacey, my love——'

It still gave her the quivers when he called her that, even though at the moment they were sleepy ones. 'Hmm?'

'Do you think we could consider having another one in a year or two?'

She thought for an instant that she was going to cry. She knew he loved Michael; how could anyone not? But still, she felt sometimes that the whole thing had been a bit unfair, and that Damon might have preferred it if she had made a different choice on that hot afternoon in Arizona.

'Oh, I think so,' she said softly.

He pulled her to her feet. 'Shall we go back to bed and discuss it? I'm only doing Michael a favour, you know. A sister, that's what he needs—then he won't have all the problems I did in figuring out how women think...'

She smiled a little, and whispered, 'I love you, Damon Kendrick.' That's such an inadequate way to say it, she thought. It's a hundred times more than that, and every day I find a new reason to love him.

'That's one of the things I still don't understand, you know,' he said.

'You don't have to understand it. Just believe it.'

He kissed her gently. 'I do, my love. I do.'

And that was the true miracle, she thought. Just loving, without doubts or questions or fears. Loving, with no reservations...

Harlequin Presents

Coming Next Month

Available in June wherever paperback books are sold, or through Harlequin Reader Service:

In the U.S.
901 Fuhrmann Blvd.
P.O. Box 1397
Buffalo, N.Y. 14240-1397

In Canada
P.O. Box 603
Fort Erie, Ontario
L2A 5X3

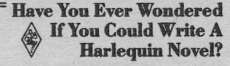

Have You Ever Wondered If You Could Write A Harlequin Novel?

Here's great news—Harlequin is offering a series of cassette tapes to help you do just that. Written by Harlequin editors, these tapes give practical advice on how to make your characters—and your story—come alive. There's a tape for each contemporary romance series Harlequin publishes.

Mail order only

All sales final

HARLEQUIN'S "BIG WIN"
SWEEPSTAKES RULES & REGULATIONS
NO PURCHASE NECESSARY TO ENTER OR RECEIVE A PRIZE

1. To enter and join the Reader Service, scratch off the metallic strips on all your BIG WIN tickets #1-#6. This will reveal the values for each sweepstakes entry number, the number of free book(s) you will receive, and your free bonus gift as part of our Reader Service. If you do not wish to take advantage of our Reader Service, but wish to enter the Sweepstakes only, scratch off the metallic strips on your BIG WIN tickets #1-#4. Return your entire sheet of tickets intact. Incomplete and/or inaccurate entries are ineligible for that section or sections of prizes. Not responsible for mutilated or unreadable entries or inadvertent printing errors. Mechanically reproduced entries are null and void.

2. Whether you take advantage of this offer or not, your Sweepstakes numbers will be compared against a list of winning numbers generated at random by the computer. In the event that all prizes are not claimed by March 31, 1992, a random drawing will be held from all qualified entries received from March 30, 1990 to March 31, 1992, to award all unclaimed prizes. All cash prizes (Grand to Sixth), will be mailed to the winners and are payable by cheque in U.S. funds. Seventh prize to be shipped to winners via third-class mail. These prizes are in addition to any free, surprise or mystery gifts that might be offered. Versions of this sweepstakes with different prizes of approximate equal value may appear in other mailings or at retail outlets by Torstar Corp. and its affiliates.

3. The following prizes are awarded in this sweepstakes: ★ Grand Prize (1) $1,000,000; First Prize (1) $25,000; Second Prize (1) $10,000; Third Prize (5) $5,000; Fourth Prize (10) $1,000; Fifth Prize (100) $250; Sixth Prize (2500) $10; ★ ★ Seventh Prize (6000) $12.95 ARV.

   ★ This Sweepstakes contains a Grand Prize offering of $1,000,000 annuity. Winner will receive $33,333.33 a year for 30 years without interest totalling $1,000,000.

   ★ ★ Seventh Prize: A fully illustrated hardcover book published by Torstar Corp. Approximate value of the book is $12.95.

   Entrants may cancel the Reader Service at any time without cost or obligation to buy (see details in center insert card).

4. This promotion is being conducted under the supervision of Marden-Kane, Inc., an independent judging organization. By entering this Sweepstakes, each entrant accepts and agrees to be bound by these rules and the decisions of the judges, which shall be final and binding. Odds of winning in the random drawing are dependent upon the total number of entries received. Taxes, if any, are the sole responsibility of the winners. Prizes are nontransferable. All entries must be received by no later than 12:00 NOON, on March 31, 1992. The drawing for all unclaimed sweepstakes prizes will take place May 30, 1992, at 12:00 NOON, at the offices of Marden-Kane, Inc., Lake Success, New York.

5. This offer is open to residents of the U.S., the United Kingdom, France and Canada, 18 years or older except employees and their immediate family members of Torstar Corp., its affiliates, subsidiaries, Marden-Kane, Inc., and all other agencies and persons connected with conducting this Sweepstakes. All Federal, State and local laws apply. Void wherever prohibited or restricted by law. Any litigation respecting the conduct and awarding of a prize in this publicity contest may be submitted to the Régie des loteries et courses du Québec.

6. Winners will be notified by mail and may be required to execute an affidavit of eligibility and release which must be returned within 14 days after notification or, an alternative winner will be selected. Canadian winners will be required to correctly answer an arithmetical skill-testing question administered by mail which must be returned within a limited time. Winners consent to the use of their names, photographs and/or likenesses for advertising and publicity in conjunction with this and similar promotions without additional compensation.

7. For a list of our major winners, send a stamped, self-addressed envelope to: WINNERS LIST c/o MARDEN-KANE, INC., P.O. BOX 701, SAYREVILLE, NJ 08871. Winners Lists will be fulfilled after the May 30, 1992 drawing date.

If Sweepstakes entry form is missing, please print your name and address on a 3" × 5" piece of plain paper and send to:

In the U.S.
Harlequin's "BIG WIN" Sweepstakes
901 Fuhrmann Blvd.
P.O. Box 1867
Buffalo, NY 14269-1867

In Canada
Harlequin's "BIG WIN" Sweepstakes
P.O. Box 609
Fort Erie, Ontario
L2A 5X3

LTY-H590

Indulge a Little
Give a Lot

A LITTLE SELF-INDULGENCE CAN DO
A WORLD OF GOOD!

Last fall readers indulged themselves with fine romance and free gifts during the Harlequin®/ Silhouette® "Indulge A Little—Give A Lot" promotion. For every specially marked book purchased, 5¢ was donated by Harlequin/ Silhouette to Big Brothers/Big Sisters Programs and Services in the United States and Canada. We are pleased to announce that your participation in this unique promotion resulted in a total contribution of *$100,000.*

*

Watch for details on Harlequin® and Silhouette®'s
next exciting promotion in September.

A BIG SISTER
can take her places

She likes that. Her Mom does too.

HARLEQUIN SUPPORTS BIG SISTERS
For more information, contact your local Big Brothers/Big Sisters agency.

BIG BROTHERS
BIG SISTERS
OF AMERICA

BIG BROTHERS/BIG SISTERS AND HARLEQUIN

Harlequin is proud to announce its official sponsorship of Big Brothers/Big Sisters of America. Look for this poster in your local Big Brothers/Big Sisters agency or call them to get one in your favorite bookstore. Love is all about sharing.

BB/BS-1A